THE
SCARLET
TIDE

STEPHEN OSBORNE

Dreamspinner Press

Published by
Dreamspinner Press
5032 Capital Circle SW
Suite 2, PMB# 279
Tallahassee, FL 32305-7886
USA
http://www.dreamspinnerpress.com/

The Scarlet Tide
© 2013 Stephen Osborne.

Cover Art
© 2013 Anne Cain.
annecain.art@gmail.com
Cover content is for illustrative purposes only and any person depicted on the cover is a model.

ISBN: 978-1-62798-230-6
Digital ISBN: 978-1-62798-229-0

Printed in the United States of America
First Edition
October 2013

For Skyler Foss.... Thanks for letting me use your middle name.

PROLOGUE

COLTON was sure there was another guy. Almost sure, anyway.

He was standing in the little area the apartment complex laughingly referred to as a kitchen, but was in reality more of an area that happened to have a stove, a sink, and a refrigerator. Colton hovered over the stove, although what he thought he was going to do to keep the meatloaf from completely drying out, he had no clue. With a sinking feeling, he opened the oven door just enough so he could see the meat sizzling within the pan inside. Yep, it wouldn't survive for much longer.

Your own fault, Colton told himself. *Why would you believe Matt would be home when he said he would?*

Things had not been good between them for weeks. Not since Matt quit his job and joined that rock band. And even that had seemed great at first. After all, who didn't want their boyfriend to become rich and famous? And the band was good. It was still early days, but already they were getting booked in some good clubs in Broadripple. And, truth be told, Colton got a vicarious thrill in telling his friends his boyfriend was in a band. Colton loved music, and it had always been the bane of his existence that he couldn't carry a tune or play an instrument himself. So who could blame him if he made it sound like Matt and his band would be opening for the Foo Fighters next tour?

Okay, they weren't that good. Not yet.

Of course, Colton didn't reveal the downside of having a boyfriend in a band to his buddies. He didn't fill them in on the late-night practices, or the promises that Matt constantly made to be home at a decent time that he never kept.

And the change that seemed to have come over Matt. Nowadays, Matt was often sullen and talked little. When he did, he seemed to find fault with nearly everything Colton did. Colton thought at first that it had been the pressure of joining an already up-and-coming band that had caused Matt's personality to do a one-eighty. Matt before the band had been sweet and loving. Still on the quiet side, but rarely argumentative and never abusive. Matt after the band *yelled.* And complained. A lot.

In the last few days, Colton had come to the conclusion that the band wasn't entirely the problem. He suspected there was someone else in Matt's life.

It would explain so much. Matt's changed behavior. How many times had Colton come into the room only to find Matt suddenly ending a conversation on his cell phone or quickly exiting out of a Facebook chat? It seemed there was nothing Colton could do that pleased Matt anymore. Matt was in love with someone else, and ready to move on.

And Colton had a good idea who it was. That little Braedon fucker. Braedon fucking Isaacs. Braedon was also in the band, the drummer, and had in fact been instrumental in getting Matt to join the group when they suddenly needed a bass player. Braedon and Matt had been friends in high school, and Colton had always suspected there was more history to the two of them than he'd ever been told.

Colton grabbed an oven mitt and pulled out the meatloaf. It looked bad. Dried out and probably tasteless. Colton's lip curled in distaste, but he set the pan on the counter and found a platter in the cupboard to transfer the meat to. At least he'd eat some of it, even if Matt couldn't be bothered to come home to enjoy it.

Colton added some vegetables to his plate and some mashed potatoes—instant, from a pouch, as it was beyond Colton's patience to make fresh for just two—and checked the kitchen clock. Two in the morning. Matt's gig was supposed to end before midnight, and he'd promised to be home well before one.

Sighing, Colton sat down at their tiny dining room table to eat by himself.

Two bites in, he heard a key fumbling in the front door lock. He almost went to greet Matt, but decided to stay put. *Allow yourself to be mad at him,* Colton told himself. *Let him know he's fucked up and you're not going to take it for much longer.*

Matt Hamilton shuffled in, his tall form clothed all in black—another new thing since joining the band—it seemed anything colorful was verboten. He looked tired and pale. Really, really pale. Worryingly pale. He slid out of his leather jacket and tossed it over a chair, his face unreadable. Colton rose quickly and went over to him, his anger melting away. Matt looked sick, or at least not his usual self. Maybe Colton had jumped to conclusions. Maybe there was a good reason for Matt's lateness. Maybe he'd imagined the whole Matt fooling around with Braedon business.

Still, Matt hadn't glanced at Colton since he'd come in. Maybe he was just feeling guilty.

"You okay?" Colton asked as he pulled Matt closer and kissed his cheek. Matt's skin felt cold. Either the temperature outside had dropped or Matt really wasn't well. Colton began to guide his boyfriend over to the table. Matt moved slowly and seemed grateful for Colton's assistance. He plopped down in the chair wearily and rubbed a hand over his face. Colton noticed the dark circles under Matt's baby blues. "You don't look well."

Matt closed his eyes and seemed to be gathering the energy to reply. His lip curled slightly as he attempted to smile. "I'm okay," he said, opening his eyelids halfway. "Just a little tired."

"I'm not surprised. You've been out every night, either playing gigs or practicing. You need a break." Colton stood behind Matt and began to rub his boyfriend's shoulders, hoping to ease some of the tension built up there.

Sighing heavily, Matt nodded at Colton's plate. "You made food," he said simply.

Colton wanted to say, "Yeah, I told you I was going to, you ass." Instead he rubbed the kinks in Matt's shoulder muscles harder. "Yeah. Meatloaf. I've had a little. It's kind of dry, but edible. Want me to get you a plate?"

Matt shook his head. "I'm not hungry. But thanks."

"You sure?" When had Colton last seen Matt eat? Weeks ago? They hadn't spent much time together lately, as Matt's band practices and gigs often went late and Colton worked days, but maybe what Matt needed was a good meal. "You must be hungry."

A touch of sadness—or at least that's how Colton interpreted the look—came to Matt's eyes. "I'll get something later," he said.

Colton ceased the kneading of Matt's shoulders and put a hand against Matt's forehead. "You don't seem to have a fever."

"I'm fine, I tell you. Just a little tired."

"Should we just head in to bed?" Colton eyed his plate hungrily. He'd purposely put off eating for hours so he could enjoy a late-night—or early morning, depending on the perspective—meal with Matt. Still, he'd had a few bites, and Matt was his first concern. How could he be so stupid to believe Matt had been cheating on him? And with that little Braedon idiot! "Let me just clear this stuff away—"

"No," Matt protested. "You eat. I'm sure you're hungry."

Colton went around and began picking up his plate and utensils. "I'm fine. I'd rather hit the sack myself. Besides, you need someone to snuggle with." He trotted to the kitchen area and deposited the remains of his meal into the trash, feeling a slight lurch in his stomach as the food slid off the plate. He returned to the table to pick up the bottle of wine he'd selected for the evening and the glasses. The wine was still corked, so they could have it another night.

"You even had wine ready for us," Matt said softly.

"More for me, I think. You've never been a connoisseur of the vine." Colton, hoping to coax a smile from Matt, held the bottle up as if he was touting the liquor for a commercial. In his best Bela Lugosi voice, he said, "I never drink... wine! But I make an exception for Woodbridge's Cabernet Sauvignon!"

He immediately regretted the jest. Matt, instead of grinning at the bad impression, seemed to tense, and his eyes flashed in anger. "Why did you do that?"

"What?" Colton was genuinely confused. Worried as well. Matt's anger had been sudden and even a little frightening. He looked like he was ready to throw Colton against the wall and belt him a few good ones. "It was only a little joke."

Matt rose so suddenly that his chair fell back, banging against the floor. His eyes were blazing as he moved close enough to Colton that their noses were nearly touching. "Well, it wasn't funny! I've had about enough of you and your stupid jokes!"

"But I—" Colton was about to explain that he hadn't meant anything by his words, but there was no need. Before he could say more, Matt spun on his heels and was down the hall in an instant. Colton heard their bedroom door slam.

Even though Matt hadn't physically touched him, Colton felt as if he'd been punched in the gut. He stood for a moment, barely daring to move, staring at the empty space where Matt had been sitting. Something was definitely wrong, and it wasn't a simple illness.

If he is fooling around with that little Braedon fucker, Colton thought, *I'll make them both regret it.* Colton wasn't by nature a fighter, and there was no way he'd win against the taller and stronger Matt if it came to blows, but he'd hunt down Braedon Isaacs and teach him a thing or two. The thought of punching Braedon in the face snapped Colton out of his stupor.

Was that what was happening, though? Up to a few weeks ago, Matt had been Matt, the Matt Colton loved. As soon as he came home and announced that he'd joined a band, though, things had changed. Since that night, Colton had hardly *seen* Matt, and when he did, they inevitably ended up arguing. Matt now slept all day and was still in bed when Colton came home from work. Colton would make something for them to eat before Matt had to rush off to rehearsal or a show or whatever, but by the time the food was cooked and Matt finally crawled out of bed, it was always too late and Matt would have to throw on some clothes—always black—and bolt out of the apartment. And when Matt finally came home, Colton was usually already in bed and asleep. Colton figured that, in the past two weeks, he'd seen Matt up and awake an hour, maybe two. Total.

He wondered if he should go in the bedroom and try to talk with Matt. Surely things weren't so bad that they couldn't discuss their relationship, or what was left of it. But the savage fury Matt had just shown over a trivial joke really worried Colton. In Colton's mind, he saw himself gently opening their bedroom door and asking if they could talk, only to be physically attacked by Matt. And Colton knew he couldn't take that, couldn't face being punched by Matt. That would be the end of it all for sure, something Colton wasn't ready for.

Unsure of what to do, Colton sat on the couch and turned on the TV. There was an old *Star Trek* episode on, one Colton had seen several times. One of the worst ones, where Kirk's body was inhabited by a woman and vice versa. It didn't matter, as Colton barely paid attention to the screen. His mind was too occupied.

Should he sleep out here on the couch, or wait until Matt was asleep and then sneak in? Neither prospect was pleasing. The couch was short and lumpy, and if he went in and Matt *wasn't* asleep, everything might explode again. Colton turned the sound down and listened. He thought he could hear movement coming from their bedroom. Matt wasn't asleep, then.

Colton switched off the set. Maybe Matt was feeling just as bad as he was. Maybe all that was needed was for one of them to make the first move, offer the first olive branch, for them to make up and forget the silly fight. Still, Colton was hesitant to enter the bedroom. Instead, he went to the bathroom across the hall from their room, and made a lot of noise preparing to brush his teeth. After all, if he could hear Matt moving around in the bedroom—what was he doing in there, pacing up and down?—then Matt could surely hear him.

Sure enough, by the time Colton had worked up the toothpaste into a lather in his mouth, the bedroom door creaked open. Colton didn't turn, but he saw Matt in the bathroom mirror, emerging wearing only a pair of basketball shorts. Colton nearly smiled when he saw the shorts were black, but he didn't want to be the first to show he wasn't mad. No, it was Matt who was acting like a jerk. *The ball's*, Colton thought, *in his court.*

But there was something wrong with the mirror. Matt was pale, true, but he looked almost translucent in the reflection. Like he was barely there. Blink, and he couldn't be seen at all. It was like the photo in one of those old *Back to the Future* movies, where Marty McFly was vanishing from the picture because he had changed the past and therefore was being removed from the future. Matt had always been pale, but this went beyond skin tone. Colton, still with a mouth full of foam, turned to look at his boyfriend. Matt was standing in the doorway, pale but substantial. It had been the mirror, after all.

Matt looked chagrined. "I guess I need to apologize."

Colton huffed and turned to the sink and spat. He turned on the faucet and bent his head down to fill his mouth with cold water. He rinsed and then spat out more foam. Straightening, he said, "You guess you need to?"

Matt came up behind him and put his hands on Colton's shoulders. "I *do* apologize. I acted like a fool. I'm—"

Colton was staring at the mirror, wondering why his lover had stopped speaking. Oddly, Colton's reflection was perfectly defined in the glass, but Matt could hardly be seen, as if he were a mere wraith standing behind Colton. Matt must have seen the anomaly as well, because he was glaring angrily at the mirror. His eyes seemed to have turned red with anger. He roughly let go of Colton's shoulders and picked up the glass that they kept their toothbrushes in. Colton ducked when he saw Matt drawing his arm back in preparation for the throw. Seconds later there was a loud crack and a shatter as the glass collided with the mirror. Colton put his hands up to his face, fearful of flying glass, but the damage didn't extend to shards scattering everywhere. There were several splinters across the mirror and a small area, right at the point of impact, where the backing of the mirror now showed. There was glass on the counter and in the sink, mostly remnants of the toothpaste glass, which seemed to have suffered more than the mirror.

"What the hell was that—" Colton didn't finish. Matt was gone. Colton heard thumping footsteps go down the hall and then the opening of the front door.

"What are you doing?" Colton yelled as he rushed out of the bathroom. "You can't go outside dressed like—" Again, he didn't complete his sentence. There was no need. Matt had slammed the door behind him. He'd gone outside in only shorts, despite it being late October. With no shoes.

Scared and confused, Colton went after him. By the time Colton got out to the parking lot, though, he heard Matt's car speeding off. Colton saw the taillights disappearing around the corner. He hadn't heard Matt pick up his keys, but they would have been in the bowl on the stand by the door where they usually were kept, so it wouldn't have been difficult for Matt to grab them, even as fast as he had to have been moving.

Colton stood there, dumbfounded. He listened until he could no longer hear the sound of Matt's engine as the car raced away. He tried to come up with some logical explanation for Matt's behavior, but none came to him. The irrational bursts of anger were troubling enough, but what was up with the mirror? If it had been some defect in the glass, then why was Colton's reflection not affected? Colton shivered, not entirely because of the cool night air. His mind raced. Drugs? Fooling around with Braedon or some other guy? Those explanations might cover the behavior, but not the mirror.

Something strange was going on, and Colton was very afraid for his lover.

CHAPTER 1

"Whoa. I feel a cold spot. Right here! Oh my God, it's like it's ten degrees colder right here!"

"Maybe," I said, trying to let Nick down gently, "it's because you're standing by a window."

Nick emitted an anguished moan as he turned and played the beam of his flashlight over the windowpane. He waved a hand in front of the glass. "You're right. It's not very well insulated. I thought the ghost was ready to make an appearance."

"They don't always pop right up. Sometimes you've got to wait for them. They don't appear on command, no matter what you see on television."

"Well," Nick said, sounding almost wistful, "not all of us have ghost radar like you do."

Whatever reply I was going to make was stopped by the feeling I suddenly got at the back of my neck. I wouldn't say I'm psychic, not as most people think of the word. I can't read minds. I can't tell you if the next card in the deck will be the queen of hearts or the ace of spades or whatever. Hell, I can't even predict the weather, a talent that seems to plague the Indianapolis weather guys as well, as they hadn't warned anyone about the sudden plunge in temperature or the accompanying rain we were enjoying. I can, however, tell if anything supernatural is lurking nearby, ready to jump out and go, "Boo." And something was preparing itself now, gathering up energy.

We had just entered the auditorium at the school where Nick taught history to a bunch of teenagers who didn't know Karl Marx from Groucho Marx. Recently, the school had started renovating the auditorium, which sometimes stirs up paranormal activity. New seats had been installed, and the plaster that had been peeling from the ceiling for years was getting a makeover. You'd think ghosts would like the places they haunt to be kept up, but they can be a pissy bunch. Since the work had begun, contractors, students, and faculty had reported seeing the apparition of a middle-aged woman with long, stringy hair and sorrowful eyes. The official word from the school's office was that it was all hogwash, but try telling that to the frightened junior who had peed herself when she turned the corner and caught sight of the specter.

"Where did this woman kill herself? Somewhere on the stage?"

Nick nodded. "Yeah. Over here." He led the way down the aisle. Every now and then, he'd slow his pace and scan the area around him with his flashlight to make sure Evelyn Banks wasn't sitting there waiting for convocation to begin.

Ms. Banks had taught art back in the '70s, or so Nick had told me. She'd also been the director of the musical the school put on every year. She had been married for four years to a man who, according to legend, loved football more than her. Ms. Banks found solace in the arms of a student, who happened to be the captain of the football team. While Evelyn Banks fell deeply in love with the student, it was merely a fling for him, a few tumbles in the hay with an older woman. When Ms. Banks learned her affections weren't returned, something snapped and she hanged herself. Over the years, the story had been embellished, and some stories even had the young man shooting himself when he discovered the body. What the guy was doing with a loaded firearm in the school auditorium is anyone's guess. Maybe the school play had been really bad that year.

We were approaching the stage area when Nick stopped short. "There's a shadow over there. I'm sure of it." He had turned to his left and was nervously checking the nearby seats.

Robbie suddenly materialized several feet in front of him. He was wearing jeans that were ripped at the knees, a wrinkled football jersey, and a cheeky grin. "And now the fun can begin," he said.

"Do you see it? The shadow?" Nick's voice had gone up an octave.

Nick was getting better at seeing ghosts, but more often than not, they were unformed shadows to him. "It's Robbie," I told him. I switched off my flashlight. There was a ghost light on stage, a single bare bulb left burning that emitted enough light for me to get around without knocking into things. "Anything?" I asked my late boyfriend.

Robbie gave the tiniest of shrugs. "She's here, but I'm sure you've already picked up on that. She's hiding, though."

Nick turned to me. "He just said something, didn't he?"

"Yeah. He said that she's here. Hanging back, but here."

Something close to a smile came to Nick's lips. "I thought I heard something. A whisper. I'm not sure if it's a good thing or not that I can almost hear him most of the time."

The more time you spend around ghosts and creepy things of all persuasions, be they demons, ghouls, or whatever the more your system gets attuned to them. I always have had the gift and grew up seeing ghosts—and other supernatural goodies—all the time, so I was used to Robbie suddenly popping up. When I became a private detective, I naturally was drawn to cases that featured otherworldly elements. You do what you're good at, what can I say? Nick, however, was still trying to adjust to the fact that there were things around him he hadn't been aware of before. I could tell he was so wired that, if he did catch sight of Ms. Banks, he would probably scream loud enough to wake the dead that weren't already up and around.

And Ms. Banks was gathering energy to make her grand appearance. The tiny hairs on the back of my neck were bristling, an indication that things were about to happen, and in a big way. Off to the side there were some steps leading up to the stage. I walked over to them slowly. Nick and Robbie followed. Nick was rubbing his arms. "It's cold in here," he muttered.

"And getting colder." I stepped onto the stage, aware of the shadows being cast by the theater's ghost light. Ghost lights have a practical use, of course. They keep people from walking off the stage into the orchestra pit when the house lights are off. But there's also the superstitious element attached to the custom of leaving a lamp burning on stage. Most theaters have at least one ghost, either actual or legendary, and the light is supposed to appease the spirits that don't like to see a darkened stage. If there were other ghosts in this theater, they were gone for the moment, fearful of the dominant and malevolent personality of Ms. Banks.

"Evelyn?" Robbie called out. "Why don't you come out and talk to us?"

At the back of the stage, I heard a soft chuckle. Not one of those "Oh aren't we having fun" chuckles. More like an "I'm going to scare the fuck out of you" chuckle. Luckily, I don't scare easily.

"Thanks for doing this, Duncan," Nick said. "I figured if anyone could get this ghost to behave, it would be you."

"No problem," I answered. The truth was, I was between cases anyway and I had nothing else to do that night, and the judging on *The X Factor* was starting to piss me off royally, so TV was out. I nodded toward the back of the stage, which was mostly vague shapes and dark shadows. "She's back there. Can you feel her?"

Nick shone the beam of his flashlight around. "I feel something. I'm not sure what."

"We're not here to hurt you," I said to the shadows, some of which seemed to be shifting. "We just want to talk. You're scaring the kids who go to school here."

"And that's so not cool," Robbie added. When I glanced at him with a raised eyebrow, he added, "Hey, I'm just trying to get her to chat. I figure I look like a student, I should use their language."

It was true; Robbie could pass for a high school kid. He'd died at the age of twenty, over a decade ago. We'd been close to the same age then. Now I was in my early thirties and getting gray hairs around my temples, while he remained fresh cheeked and youthful. It was a pisser, as every time I looked in the mirror, I wondered how much longer the two of us could go on like we were. His dying really put a crimp in our relationship. Especially as... well, we won't even talk about our sex life. Mainly because there wasn't one.

My thoughts were interrupted by a sudden breeze that shot across the stage. The gust was enough to ruffle my hair. At the back of the stage there was now a white light. It started off as just a speck but quickly grew and formed a human shape. Ms. Banks was ready to receive visitors, and she wasn't happy we were there.

She was thin and fairly tall, wearing black slacks and a gray top. Her hair hung down limply to her shoulders and her dark eyes burned with hatred. Seconds after she materialized, she let out a wail and moved with inhuman speed, shooting downstage toward us with arms outstretched.

Ms. Banks must have summoned enough energy that even Nick could see her, because he yelled out, "Shit!" The ghost had been aiming for me, but seeing that she had a better audience—and a more nervous one—she veered toward Nick instead. He backpedaled several paces and would have fallen into the pit if Robbie hadn't sucked in energy to become solid enough to grab Nick by the elbow. The spirit of Evelyn Banks went right through Nick and shot out over the orchestra pit and into the seating area. She was floating several feet off the ground, sailing right over the seats. Her laughter echoed throughout the theater. Halfway up the aisle, she vanished.

Nick put a hand over his heart as if to quell the rapid beating. "Holy fuck," he said, his voice shaking, "she went right through me!"

"Yeah, something seems to have annoyed her." I went over to him and put a hand on his shoulder. "You okay?"

"I think so. Was that Robbie that grabbed me?"

Robbie grimaced. "Oh yeah, sure. Spooky McPhee he can see. Me, I'm still the Invisible Man."

I nodded. "Yeah, it was Robbie. Be careful. I think she was trying to get you to fall off the stage."

"I thought you said ghosts usually didn't try to harm people."

"Usually not, but this one's nuttier than my Aunt Sally's fruitcake." I didn't actually have an Aunt Sally, nor was I sure if there were even nuts in fruitcake, but it seemed a good idea to keep things light in tone so Nick didn't freak out. "I'm not sure we can convince her to play nice."

"So we go to Plan B?" Nick asked.

"Not yet. Let's give her one more chance." I turned to my spectral boyfriend. "Robbie? Think you can find her and have a nice ghost-to-ghost chat?"

He nodded. "On it," he said as he promptly vanished.

The atmosphere in the theater had changed now that Ms. Banks wasn't rearing her angry head. Everything seemed very calm and peaceful. I sat down on the edge of the stage and let my legs dangle. Nick walked around for a few minutes, scanning every nook and cranny with his flashlight. His own step made a floorboard creak, and he nearly jumped out of his skin. I patted the area next to me.

"Come and sit down. She's not here right now. Let's see if Robbie can get to her act sensibly."

Nick hovered for a moment but finally decided that pacing wasn't accomplishing anything, so he sat down next to me. We were quiet for nearly a minute until he broke the silence. "I screamed like a little girl, didn't I?"

"It was a manly scream. Chuck Norris would have been proud."

Nick laughed uneasily. "I nearly peed myself."

"Nearly is good. It's when you follow through that a change of underwear is needed." I put my arm around his shoulder. "Honestly, you did good. Seeing something like that coming at you, howling like a banshee, would make almost anyone scream like a little girl."

"Oh, so I *did* scream like a girl."

"A very butch little girl. Don't be so hard on yourself."

It felt odd, having my arm around Nick. A while ago, when I'd been having doubts about my relationship with Robbie—after all, he was dead—I'd sort of dated Nick. It didn't go far, but he'd become a good friend and had stuck around through thick and thin. Touching him, though, brought thoughts into my head I didn't want there. I removed the hand.

Nick may have felt uncomfortable with the contact as well because he cleared his throat loudly and shifted ever so slightly away from me. "Do you think Robbie can get through to her? I don't want to get rid of her if she wants to be here, as long as she doesn't scare the bejesus out of everyone."

"We'll do what we can," I said, although I wasn't feeling optimistic. The look I'd seen in her eyes was that of sheer madness. If we let her go on, someone was going to get hurt.

"If we banish her—is that the right word?—what actually happens to her?"

I sighed. "I don't really know." And that was the truth. "Getting ghosts to move on is not really my area of expertise. If you believe that jerk on TV, though, that Ricky Vallis, they go onto a better place." On a case not too long ago, I'd run into the host of the paranormal show *I See Dead People.* I hated him from the start, and didn't see eye to eye with him in matters pertaining to ghosts, but a lot of people hung on his every word. "I hope that's true, and that if they go willingly, they go to Heaven or Valhalla or Sto-vo-kor or Happy Bunny Land or wherever. Banished spirits I'm not so sure about. There's a different feel in the air when you banish a ghost. It feels like you're killing them. Hard to do, when they're already dead, but you know what I mean."

Nick nodded sagely and then looked at me questioningly. "Sto-vo-kor?"

"The Klingon equivalent to Heaven. I've been watching a lot of *Deep Space Nine* lately."

That got a laugh. "You really don't know what to do with yourself when you're not on a case."

"True."

Another silence followed. Where the hell was Robbie? How long could it possibly take to convince a nasty and possibly insane ghost to either move on or at least stop being such a butt? Okay, maybe quite a while, but didn't he know the silence was getting awkward between me and Nick?

Nick, looking out over the rows and rows of seats and very definitely not at me, finally said, "I met a guy the other night."

"Oh?"

"At that bar I like. The one where you and I met. Nice guy. I got his phone number. We had a really great chat."

"That's great," I said, struggling to keep my voice even. Why was this like getting bad news? I should be feeling happy for my friend. Instead, I felt like someone had kicked me in the gut. Did I really expect Nick to remain single for all time, my backup plan just in case something happened between me and Robbie?

"I'm thinking about calling him. Not right now, of course. Tomorrow. Ask him out."

"You should."

Nick looked at me. "You think I should?"

I swallowed, which wasn't easy, as my mouth seemed to be suddenly devoid of saliva. "Yeah. I think you should."

Nick's gaze went back to the rows of seats. "You know, if things had been—"

I never heard what the things were or anything about them, because at that moment, Robbie appeared. He materialized in running mode, belting down the aisle toward us as if he was being chased by all the Hounds of Hell, which in a way he was. "She's really pissed off now!" he exclaimed, darting a backward look.

Behind him, the cackling spirit of Evelyn Banks suddenly formed, zooming after him several feet off the ground. Black ooze was now dripping out of her mouth and eye sockets, and her outstretched hands were cracked and gnarled, more like the hands of an aged crone than that of a young schoolteacher.

I quickly stood and pulled my cell phone out of my pocket. I hit the button that speed dialed my best friend, Gina. When she answered, I just said, "Now."

"Okay" was Gina's reply.

Robbie vaulted over the railing and leaped into the orchestra pit. The howling, screaming spirit of Ms. Banks sailed over him and toward Nick and me. She slowed her pace, wanting to approach us in as menacing a manner as possible. Her form even seemed to grow, her features distorting like the reflection of a carnival mirror. Nick, alarmed, scrambled backward. The specter seemed to delight in Nick's terror as a grin spread across her cracked lips, which also sent more black goo dribbling down her chin.

The grin froze suddenly, and a worried look came into the apparition's eyes. Evelyn Banks stopped moving as she realized something was wrong. She looked down at her body, which was rapidly being consumed by blue flame. She shrieked, the sound reverberating loudly in the auditorium. Soon she was simply a ball of fire, and then only a few blackened bits of ash hanging in the air. Even the ash vanished before it floated to the floor.

"Plan B," I said, pocketing my cell phone. "Works every time."

Nick was very, very pale and seemed to be having a hard time remembering to breathe. "Yeah. I like Plan B. Nice plan. One of my favorites."

Robbie slowly rose from the orchestra pit, sailing up through the air until he was level with the stage. Once there, he calmly stepped forward until his feet were on solid wood. "Plan B only works, though, if you have someone standing by the spirit's grave ready to give them the old zapperoo."

Robbie generally didn't do the hovering trick, as it consumed too much energy, but I suppose he wanted to show that he was just as good at it as Banks had been. "Like the Boy Scouts, it's best to come to these things prepared."

Finding out where Evelyn Banks had been buried hadn't been too difficult. The hard part had been actually locating her grave, as she was buried in Crown Hill Cemetery, the largest burial spot in Indianapolis. True, we could have gone to the folks at Crown Hill and asked them to check their records, and they could have provided a handy map for us showing Evelyn's plot, but I thought we should leave them out of it if possible. After all, Gina would have to be waiting at the grave, possibly for hours, and I didn't want to call any more attention to Evelyn Banks's final resting place than necessary.

Not that Gina had to disturb the grave in order to kibosh Banks's spirit. As a healing witch, all Gina had to do was kneel over the grave and run some of the dirt from the plot through her fingers while doing an incantation. Saves all that digging and burning the bones. So messy. Also, it's very hard to explain to the police what you're doing in a cemetery at night with a shovel. They frown on that sort of thing. Can't imagine why.

Witches, despite what you may have seen on television or in the movies, don't just twitch their nose and—poof!—some guy's a cat! They generally have powers that come naturally to them, such as levitation, transmogrification, or mental manipulation. Gina's specialty was healing. Over the years, she'd picked up a few other useful spells and magicks, but generally she was a healer. Which, since I seem to always be getting shot or pushed off balconies, was something that came in handy.

I kept an eye on Nick, who was starting to get a little color back to his cheeks, or at least from what I could see by the ghost light on stage. Poor guy. He hadn't asked to be thrown into this crazy life of mine. It was bad enough dealing with me, who could see ghosts and sensed whenever anything spooky was around, but he also had to deal with the fact that my boyfriend was still around after being dead for more than a decade, and that my best friend was a centuries-old witch. Oh yeah. And my bulldog, Daisy, was a zombie. But other than that, I was pretty sure I was a good friend to have. True, if Nick had never met me, he'd be a happy history teacher who rarely had malevolent spirits attacking him, instead of the shaking wreck that was standing on the stage now, but you can't have everything in this life. I went over to him and plucked at his sleeve.

"Come on. Let's go get a burger."

He blinked. "I'm not sure I could eat anything."

"Best thing for you, after having a spirit go through you. Replenish any energy that they stole from you."

Groaning, he muttered, "She stole energy from me?"

I smiled. "Come on. Burger with gloppy cheese. My treat."

Nick seemed to snap out of his paralysis and walked with me to the steps leading to the auditorium. After a few paces, he didn't even look like he was ready to collapse and fall to the floor in a heap. Robbie, with a shrug, tagged along behind us. "So," Nick said, after clearing his throat, "is this what you do most nights?"

I thought about that a moment. "When there's nothing good on TV."

CHAPTER 2

COLTON YATES had a deer in the headlights quality about him. If I said "boo" suddenly, he seemed like he'd bolt from the room, possibly screaming. He wore jeans that had seen better days, a red T-shirt that really didn't go with his freckled complexion, and scuffed canvas tennis shoes. He'd told me he was twenty-one, and I had no reason to doubt him, but I would have put him at seventeen or eighteen, tops. Could have been the freckles, though, which gave him an Opie Taylor quality, if Opie had had darker hair and a couple tattoos. Colton had two I could see. On his right wrist was a blue star. On his left was Wile E. Coyote from the Warner Brothers cartoons.

Overall, he didn't strike me as one of the wealthiest clients who'd ever sat across the desk from me, but what the hell. I liked Wile E. Coyote too. You have to give a predator snaps for being that persistent.

He looked like he hadn't slept in days, and eating hadn't been a high priority either. He was a skinny cuss. I'm not a weight lifter, but even I wouldn't have much trouble bench pressing the kid. He must have realized I was taking stock of him, because he bit his lip and looked down at his shoes.

"I suppose I'd better say right off the bat that I don't have a lot of money, so if you charge a lot—"

If he'd been looking up, he'd have seen my patented reassuring smile. "Why don't you tell me about what's troubling you first. We can worry about the money angle later."

He looked at me and tried to smile. "I was hoping you'd say that. I just… I just didn't know what else to do."

I waited. I thought the silence might be a signal for him to continue, but instead he fidgeted in his chair. I went for the reassuring smile and calming tone of voice. Killer combination. "Go on."

Colton was still reluctant. "I'd heard that you sometimes deal with strange stuff. Stuff no one else even believes in."

Ah, the price of fame. I'd have to add that to my business card, putting *Dealer in Strange Stuff* right under *Private Detective*. "Sometimes," I said.

"I went to this psychic guy last night. I thought he might be able to tell me where Matt is, but he couldn't. But he told me to come to you."

Wise psychic, and that's not something I say very often. Most of the ones I've met are full of hooey. It didn't take psychic powers on my part to see this Matt and Colton were an item, however. There was that combination of worry and longing in Colton's eyes that spoke of a missing lover.

Colton went on. "Matt's my boyfriend. Or at least, he was." He paused and looked at me as if waiting for me to frown or throw up my hands in disgust, or at least chuckle derisively. Oh, those homos. Thinking they can love each other. I gathered that Colton and Matt had not had an easy time with someone. Probably family. When I merely smiled encouragingly, Colton said, "We've been living together for almost a year now."

"Good for you guys," I said, meaning it. I'm all for young love, unless it involves someone named Edward and a girl named Bella. Then they should be flogged.

"I wish my mom thought that way. She barely speaks to me anymore."

Bingo. Was I good or what? Family. "How does Matt's family feel about it?" I asked. It seemed like I should say something.

"Oh, they're really cool. Well, his brother is a bit of an asshole, but his mom's great. She's helped us out a lot. Got us some old furniture when we moved in together. Stuff like that."

"So what's happened with Matt?"

"I think he's possessed." Colton stared at me, looking to see if I'd burst out laughing or roll my eyes. When I did neither, he went on. "He's not the same anymore. These last few weeks, he's been like someone else. Someone I don't know." Now that it was out of his mouth, his eyes brimmed with tears. When they started to fall, I pushed a box of tissues closer to him. Colton pulled one out, wiped his eyes, and then blew his nose. It sounded like a lot of snot exited his tiny, upturned schnoz. He took a deep breath and flushed with embarrassment. "Sorry about that, but I just don't know what to do."

"There's a lot we can do, actually," I told him. "The first thing, though, is that we have to see if your boyfriend really is possessed."

"He is," Colton said, his voice cracking. "What else could it be?"

Drugs, for one, but Colton had probably already considered that and discarded the idea. He seemed like a bright young man. "Do you live with Matt?" Dumb question. The kid already said they had furniture. Where did I think they kept it, in their cars? But I was going for calm and gently easing Colton into his story, and dumb questions sometimes work.

He nodded. "At least, I did. I haven't seen him for two days." He took another tissue and blew his nose. When he finished, he muttered, "Sorry."

"No need to be. Why don't you give me the details. Why do you think Matt's possessed?"

Colton had two used tissues wadded up in his left hand. Before speaking, he glanced around for a wastebasket. Finding one, he tossed them inside. Then he began, "Everything was fine before he joined that band. He used to work at Taco Bell as a shift leader."

Colton had that look I'd seen all too often. The look said, *I've come here, but now I don't think I can say what's really troubling me.* I tried the reassuring smile again. "Go on."

"A few weeks ago his friend Braedon convinced him to join this band, a rock band...." He reached into the pocket of his jeans and pulled out a folded piece of paper. He handed it to me.

I unfolded the sheet and saw it was a flier for a performance at a club in Broadripple, by a group called The Scarlet Tide. There was a photo of the group. Three guys and one girl, all of them wearing black.

"That's Matt on the left," he said.

Tall, weedy, angry looking. He didn't look like he matched up with a nice kid who had a tattoo of Wile E. Coyote above his wrist. He didn't look possessed to me, just pissed off. But you can't always tell from a photograph. Something else worried me more. When Colton had passed me the flier, I had noticed some red marks on his wrist. Bite marks, either from a particularly nasty insect, or something worse.

I tried to look nonchalant. No reason to make him freak out any more than he already was. "What happened to your wrist?"

He looked at the marks, two punctures a few inches apart. "This? I don't know. Mosquitoes, I think."

"Few mosquitoes in October. And you rarely get mosquitoes that vicious. Those look nasty. When did you first notice them?"

He frowned, thinking. "Just this morning. Why?"

"Probably not important. So how has Matt been acting that's so different from normal?"

Colton took a deep breath, and then plunged in. Once he committed to telling his story, the words just poured out. He gave it all to me. The irrational behavior. The fights. The strange reflection in the mirror. "Can you help me?"

"Yeah. Yeah, I can help you."

Colton almost smiled. I could tell he'd been waiting for me to laugh hysterically or throw him out, calling him a loony. "Thanks."

"But," I said. His eyes went big in anticipation. "But you have to trust me."

"Okay."

"You've got to be absolutely truthful with me. I've got some questions for you. First is this." I held up the band's flier. "According to this, Matt and The Scarlet Tide have been playing at this club for the last two nights. I'm guessing you haven't gone to see him. Why not?"

"I don't know," he answered. He saw I wouldn't let that reply stand, so he went on. "I guess I was a little afraid to go. You didn't see the look in his eyes when he smashed the mirror. I thought he was going to kill me."

I nodded. "Now, tell me about any dreams you've had in the past few days."

That shocked him. "What?"

"Specifically last night."

Colton bit his lip, then said, "Just weird nightmare stuff. I haven't been sleeping well."

"Uh-huh. But did one of your nightmares involve seeing Matt again?"

Again the eyes went to saucer-like proportions. "I.... I didn't...." Colton sighed. "It was just a fucked-up dream. You know how dreams are."

"I need to hear it. Trust me."

He shuffled his feet around a bit and then crossed his legs. That didn't seem to work, so he uncrossed them and did a bit more fidgeting. "It was kind of a sex dream. He came into the bedroom. I was already in bed. He took off his clothes and got into bed with me and we started making out. Do you really want to hear this?"

Hell, if he knew how my sex life was, he wouldn't ask. I have to know there are some people in the world who have a normal sex life. "It's important."

"We were getting hot and heavy, kissing and fondling and stuff. And then...." Colton sighed.

"He bit you."

Colton nodded.

"Right on the wrist. Right where you have those marks."

Again, he nodded.

"You know it wasn't really a dream, don't you?"

Colton closed his eyes. "I thought I was going crazy. I mean, that's movie stuff. Stuff like that doesn't really happen. It's just crazy."

"I'm good with crazy. Deal with it all the time."

He laughed without mirth. "Yeah, but this crazy? I don't know why I'm here. There's nothing you can do for me. I should probably see a shrink."

"I can do something for you." The kid snorted, but a gleam of hope showed in his eyes. "You're not crazy."

"So you can help me? Me and Matt?"

I could help Colton. Matt was beyond my help. The only thing I could do was to destroy the thing he'd become.

CHAPTER 3

I'M NOT a big fan of Halloween. Dealing with ghosts, demons, and other nasties on a regular basis, it just seems a bit excessive to me. A little kid showing up at my door in a bad Bela Lugosi mask and sporting a diminutive cape, wanting me to hand him some candy, often gets more than he bargained for. Daisy, my dog, not only barks up a storm, but the sight of her often sends a shiver or two up the youngster's spine. She doesn't look bad, for a zombie bulldog anyway. She has a grayish tint to her skin, and her fur has a look to it that's a little off, but you can't exactly say why. The bloodshot, slightly bulging eyes are what get the little tykes. Plus, most kids can see ghosts, at least in some form or other, so Robbie often sends them screaming, especially if they see a half-formed figure standing behind me while I'm passing out the goodies. Most of the neighborhood kids have figured out it's best to bypass our place.

The holiday was still days away, but the apartment next to ours was having a party, and loads of kids in costume were traipsing past our door to join the revelries in 2C. A few, either from excitement or from their parents getting the apartment number wrong, had already knocked on our door by mistake, so when I'd just gotten settled on the couch next to Daisy and was disturbed by a *thump, thump, thump*, I figured it would be another dinky Spider-Man or living skeleton. Instead I found Gina standing out in the hall.

"Trick or treat," she said with a smile.

I let her in. Daisy, who quickly recognized a friend, stopped her barking and went back to the couch to settle in for a well-deserved nap. I took Gina's black cloak and hung it on the rack.

You'd think Gina would opt to wear clothes that didn't make people think of a modern-day witch, considering she is one.

She went the other way, wearing lots of flowing black garments. Stick a pointy hat on her and buckle shoes, and the picture would be complete. Far from an old hag with a wart on her nose, though, Gina appeared to be young and blonde, even though she'd been born several centuries ago. She probably has a good moisturizing regime.

"What brings you out tonight?" I asked.

She brushed at her sleeve. It must have started to sprinkle outside, for there were traces of droplets on the black fabric. "Didn't Nick tell you?"

"Nick? He didn't say anything to me. He did mention that he was going to stop by tonight, but I figured he just wanted to watch a movie or something."

"He called me earlier, asked if I could come by. Said there was something he wanted me to do for him before I left."

Gina had never taken a vacation in all the years I'd known her, but had decided to take a two-week jaunt with her boyfriend, Mark the Dentist. They were going to Gina's childhood hometown of Salem, Massachusetts, and the purpose of the journey was that Gina had decided it was time to let Mark know the person he was dating was a healing witch. She was understandably nervous about the trip and the reaction of a regular Joe finding out the gal he was dating had known Mary Todd Lincoln personally. Well, Gina told me she did, and I had no way of contradicting her.

"Nick's been acting odd since the other night," I told her. She raised a questioning eyebrow, so I explained, "He had an angry spirit pass through him. Kind of freaked him out."

"It has that effect on people. Speaking of odd, where's Robbie?"

I scanned the room, half expecting him to materialize. When he didn't, I said, "He's here, just storing up some energy."

"He's been doing a lot of that lately," she stated simply.

It was true. Robbie was spending more and more time where even I couldn't see or hear him, in the ghost equivalent of sleep. As a result, I'd been spending more time with Nick the last few weeks. I wondered if I was getting into some weird relationship Möbius loop where I spent time with Nick because of Robbie's absences, but then Robbie stayed away more because I was spending time with Nick. Maybe I was just overthinking things. Every relationship goes through its ups and downs, even when one of the people in the relationship died in a car crash ten years ago.

A knock at the door let me push aside these thoughts. When I opened it, it wasn't Nick like I expected, but a little girl dressed as a princess, with a confused-looking mother standing behind her. "I think we've got the wrong apartment, Cindy," Mom said with an apologetic look at me.

The kid was looking past me, at Gina. Daisy remained on the couch, apparently having decided there had been too many visitors at our door that night to warrant further barking. Gina had been adjusting the many charms that dangled from chains around her neck, and finally felt the tiny eyes on her. She turned.

"Aren't you a pretty princess," Gina told the kid.

The girl was indeed a charmer. She half closed her right eye, and I thought at first she was trying to squint at Gina, but then I saw that she had some sort of eye infection. "Are you a witch?" the kid asked.

Gina bent down to kid level. "I am," she said in a stage whisper, as if revealing a deep, dark secret. Which, in truth, she was. "What's wrong with your eye?"

"I gots a stye."

The mother looked embarrassed. "Come on, honey. We need to find the right apartment. No need to bother these people."

Gina reached out a hand and placed her forefinger on the kid's half-closed eye. She muttered something under her breath, and the princess's eye glowed green for the merest of seconds before returning to normal. I looked at the mother. "You need 2C, down the hall," I told her.

Kid and mom went away, and I shut the door. Gina was grinning.

"Won't mom find it odd that the kid's eye cleared up once Witchy Woman touched it?" I asked.

Gina shrugged. "She won't even notice until later, and by then she'll just think it cleared up on its own. Besides, I could hardly let a beautiful princess go to a party with a stye."

We were still by the door, and there was much rustling and commotion out in the hall as more kids made it down to 2C. Muffled laughter could be heard, and the party must have started in earnest as someone cranked up the stereo and the strains of Bobby "Boris" Pickett's old chestnut "The Monster Mash" came through the walls. When the door was once again rapped upon, I fully expected it to be another displaced partygoer. This time it was Nick.

He was wearing tan pants, a dark-blue polo shirt, a leather coat, and a sheepish grin. He wiggled his fingers at me. A tiny Batman, werewolf, and an accurate Matt Smith version of the Doctor from *Doctor Who* hurried down the hall behind him, followed by a full-sized and harried parent. "Looks like I'm missing the party," Nick said.

"Come on in. It's loud enough you can enjoy it without actually being there."

I got Nick inside and took his coat. Daisy, annoyed that she wasn't getting enough attention—or maybe she didn't like the Halloween novelty songs spilling through the walls—decided to get up and sniff at the cuffs of Nick's pants. He reached down and gave her a scratch between the ears. "Do you smell my cats?" Daisy sneezed by way of answer.

Nick had two cats. One he'd had for years, and one I'd given him that had been given to me by a client who couldn't keep it any longer. I hadn't wanted to worry the client at the time, so I didn't say I personally wouldn't be able to keep their feline, as I had a bulldog whose usual meal was biting the heads off squirrels, and I didn't want to tempt fate and find out the hard way that Daisy found kitty brains a delicacy.

After some debate, the three of us decided on wine, and while I found a bottle and proceeded to open it, I asked, "So what's all the mystery, Nick? Or did you want to get us all together for a game of *Clue?* Because if that's the case, I have to warn you. Gina cheats."

Gina accepted the glass I handed her. "I do not. You just really suck at board games. You never pay attention."

Nick took his wine and downed half of it in one go. "I have a favor to ask you guys. Well, another one. Zapping the ghost at our school was a pretty big one."

"We're big on doing favors. What did you have in mind?" I asked.

We had to wait for Nick to swallow more wine, and I topped up his glass. Finally, he looked at Gina. "Could you make it so that I could see ghosts? See them properly, I mean."

I'm not sure whose eyes got bigger, mine or Gina's. She set her wine down on an end table and perched on an armchair, giving her time to formulate her reply. "I could, of course. It would only take opening up parts of your mind that are filtered and aren't used often. That's putting it simply, but you get what I mean. I can do it. I'm just not sure it would be a good thing. I'm curious, though. Why do you want to be able to see ghosts?"

Nick sat down on the couch, clutching his glass like a life preserver. "I've thought about it a lot. And after the other night, when that ghost went right through me.... I just feel it's something I need to do."

I frowned. "That ghost the other night scared the shit out of you."

"I know. And seeing her did something to me. You said that the reason I saw her clearly was because she was channeling so much anger and hatred, right?" He looked at me. I nodded. "What if someone had talked to her before she became that way? When her ghost was young, so to speak. Maybe it was years of no one paying attention to her that made her start acting up and trying to frighten everyone."

"She killed herself. I'm guessing she was insane when she died. Insane people make for insane ghosts."

Nick seemed to see the logic in this, but he wasn't to be deterred. "Still, there must be others that just need encouragement to move on. You can't do it. You're busy with your cases, killing monsters and whatnot. This is something I could do to help out."

I plopped down next to him. "It's a nice thought, Nick. It really is. But there are mediums out there, real ones, who do that sort of thing."

"It seems to me that there's a shortage on mediums and an overabundance of ghosts."

He had me there. Still, I shook my head. "You don't know what you're asking. Believe me, I know. Ghosts can be anywhere. You could be at your local supermarket and there will be one by the lemons or something. I see them so often I don't even give them much of a thought anymore unless they seem in distress or are causing mischief."

His face was determined. "I want to do this. I can help. I know I can."

"Even when you can't see them, you feel them. You won't have a day where you don't know that there's some deceased soul around you."

Nick, realizing he wasn't getting any support from me, turned to Gina. "Will you do it?"

She sighed. "If I do, and I'm not saying I will, you do realize that I'll be on vacation for the next few weeks. I won't be able to undo it until I get back."

"I've already made up my mind," Nick said.

Gina's shoulders raised a fraction and then lowered again. "Okay, then."

I stared at her. "What?"

"He's made his decision, Duncan."

"It's a shitty decision. Can I speak to you for a moment in the kitchen, Gina?"

We went around the corner to the relative seclusion of the kitchen, leaving Nick giving a back rub to Daisy, who sighed the absolutely contented sigh only dogs seem capable of. Standing near the refrigerator, we were out of sight of Nick but certainly not out of earshot, so we had to speak in whispers. I went first. "Have you gone out of your ever-loving mind?"

"He's got a point, Duncan. There are a lot of souls out there who need guidance, and very few people who can truly communicate with them. Most can only make their presence known by a few knocks or making an EMF detector light up like a Christmas tree if some ghost-hunting group happens along. And Nick's right, you've got bigger fish to fry. Maybe he can help out." I opened my mouth to protest further, but she cut me off. "I know what you're going to say. He'll have one hell of a time adjusting, but if he is serious about this—"

"He doesn't know what he's asking. Nick just feels left out right now. Because of me being stupid, he's been dragged into our weird little lives, and now he thinks he wants to be part of the weirdness."

"Um... I can still kind of hear you guys," Nick said from the living room.

"We'll be right with you!" Gina bellowed. To me, she said, "What, you think you should have the monopoly on seeing ghosts?"

"It's not that and you know it."

Gina really lowered her voice. If Nick could hear her now, he had Superman hearing and didn't need any more special powers. "Let him try it while I'm gone. Two weeks, Duncan. I can always cloud that part of his mind again when I get back."

I still thought it was as bad an idea as introducing Jar-Jar Binks into the *Star Wars* universe, but I could see I was outvoted. But I hated to give in. "He's getting used to being involved with the supernatural. Eventually, his system will be so attuned that he'll be able to see them on his own. Naturally. If we give him the Old Witchy Zap and turn it on all of a sudden, it's going to be hard on him. Really hard."

Gina frowned. "That's true. Maybe I can just open up his mind a little, make it a gradual process."

We turned to find Nick standing just a few feet away from us. Damn, the guy could move quietly when he wanted to. "I'm not a child," he said. His tone was a little petulant, which sounded childish to me, but I wasn't about to start an argument over that. "Guys, I've thought about this. I'm sure it's the right thing to do. I can help out. I know I can. Let me."

Gina looked at me. I could tell she was resigned to at least give him a trial run, so to speak. I sighed. I still didn't like it, but I nodded.

We returned to the living room and Gina asked Nick to sit in the armchair she'd been in. She then stood behind him and placed her fingers on his temples.

"Relax," she said.

Nick frowned. "Is it going to hurt?"

"No, but if you're nervous, you mind gets filled with a jumble of images and it makes it harder for me to find... ah, here we go." Her fingers moved in small circles over his skin. She closed her eyes momentarily and then opened them. "Done."

"Really?" Nick leaned forward as she removed her hands. "I don't feel any different. In fact, I—" He blinked and rubbed the back of his neck. "That's strange. I don't know how to describe it, but I suddenly know that something is coming." He looked at me. "Robbie?"

"Yep. You're getting what he calls my Spidey sense. It's a sort of ghost alert."

"Did someone mention my name?" Robbie materialized, wearing black basketball shorts and a gray tank top, looking like he'd just woken from a long sleep. His dark hair was tousled, and he was moving his mouth around as if adjusting it and getting the saliva evenly distributed. He rubbed his eyes and then noticed all eyes in the room were on him. "What?" he asked. "Do I have something in my teeth?"

Nick was perched so precariously on the edge of his seat that it was an even-money bet that any second he'd be on the floor. His face was pale. "That's Robbie?" he asked.

Robbie blinked, then looked at Gina and then Nick and then me. "He can see me?"

I nodded. "Yep."

"Holy shit. I hate it when I miss all the good stuff. What's been going on?"

Nick seemed to have a hard time getting his mouth to work properly. "Wow. I can see him. I mean, really see him. Not just a shadow or a vague shape. It's like he's a real person standing there!"

"Hey! Ghosts are people too!" Robbie frowned in annoyance.

"Wow." Nick repeated. "Wow. I don't know… wow."

"Surprised at how hot I look?" Robbie said with a grin.

Nick looked at me. "He looks really young. Younger than I thought." Then his face fell. I knew what was going on in his head. After all, Robbie had always been a rival of sorts to Nick, and now he was seeing him, really seeing him. And Robbie, for all his faults and foibles, was damn good-looking.

"Really, really young," Nick said.

Robbie shuffled his feet, clearly embarrassed. "I'm starting to feel like a blossoming Kate Moss here. Can everyone find something else to ogle for a moment?"

"Really, really young," Nick continued to stare and comment.

I sighed. And felt old.

CHAPTER 4

THE Adams Mansion, in the south suburb of Beech Grove, had long been known as one of the most haunted houses in the area. Some years ago, the local Jaycees had started up a haunted house attraction there that ran through the month of October, featuring volunteers dressed up as Freddy Krueger, werewolves, vampires, zombies, and what have you. I'd never been there personally. I avoid places that are known to be haunted on principle. I figure, if there really are ghosts running around the place, it's like work for me and I don't need the aggravation. On the other hand, on the few times I have been to a supposedly haunted site and found nothing, I've always gone away slightly disappointed. It's like going to Dairy Queen and discovering they're out of ice cream.

I knew I was in for trouble when I went to park my car, and couldn't find a spot within several blocks of the mansion. The sun was rapidly dipping below the horizon and the evening chill bit through my leather jacket as I walked down the sidewalk. A young couple hurried past me, hand in hand. The guy, a thin teen with a badly hooked nose, actually collided with my side in his haste to get around me. Maybe he felt my gun in the shoulder holster as he knocked against me, or maybe he was just amazed I didn't fall to the ground from the impact of his 135-pound frame, but he looked back and said he was sorry before he and his girl traveled on. The girl giggled. The boy regained his composure and let out a laugh. They obviously were on their way to the Adams Haunted House attraction and wanted to get a good place in line.

Not caring about the line, I took my time. The kids raced on, and as I watched them, I used my Sherlock Holmes detective skills on them. The boy was fifteen or so and thought he was tough. Saying sorry as he had to me wasn't something that came easily to him. His jeans were well worn and his jacket much too thin for the weather, but if you asked him, he'd reply he didn't feel the cold much. Because he was tough. But really because he couldn't afford a new jacket. The girl was the same age. Part of her was feeling all grown up—she had a tattoo on her wrist that could be barely seen peeking out of the frayed cuff of her jacket—and part was still clinging to her childhood—her jacket had a Hello Kitty on the back. Her hair was dyed a deep red to show that she, too, was tough. Both of them would go through the Haunted House laughing to show they weren't scared. Frankly, I didn't buy it.

They disappeared around the corner, and I thought about my reason for going to the Adams Mansion. Colton Yates was one of the volunteers there, and I was meeting him before his stint as a zombie. I had told him I wanted to touch base with him before heading out to watch his boyfriend's band perform, but the real reason was that I wanted to make sure old Matt hadn't been drinking any more of his blood. I hadn't yet put a stake into the heart of a client, and I didn't want Colton to be my first. I also had to let him know he wouldn't be seeing his boyfriend again, if all went as planned. When Colton had been in my office, I hadn't had the heart to inform him Matt was too far gone to save. But now that I was setting out to stake the vamp, I had to be honest with him.

Another reason for starting my night's work early was to give myself time to think. Nick's assessment of Robbie hadn't come as a surprise to me, but had niggled at me nonetheless. I was in my early thirties. Robbie would always look twenty. I would get older and older and he'd remain ageless. Not a revelation as we'd been battling that aspect of our relationship for years, but it still made me realize that at some point Robbie and I would have to decide if we were only fooling ourselves or not.

I loved him. That wasn't in question. I always would. And if he ever moved on, I'd be crushed. But eventually I'd move on as well, and maybe I'd find someone else. Maybe Nick. Maybe someone else. It would be nice in a way to date someone who I could have a physical relationship with as well. Someone I could touch and actually feel his skin on mine. Robbie could get up enough ghostly mojo so we could, on occasion, kiss, but that was about it. And I told myself that was enough, that all I needed was his love and a kiss on the lips once in a while, but maybe that was bullshit and I was just rationalizing.

Hell, I'd just fuck up a relationship with an actual breathing person anyway.

I turned the corner and came within sight of the house, and nearly cussed out loud. The line to get into the place was already long, snaking from the front door of the house and down the sidewalk to the wrought-iron fence surrounding the property, and halfway down the block. Luckily, I wasn't getting into the queue, but I wondered if I could locate Colton and chat with him before the Jaycees opened up the doors to let the masses in, and Colton would have to do his zombie act.

There were a few catcalls as I walked to the front of the line, which I ignored. While it would be fun to respond to a kid saying, "Hey, buddy, the end of the line is back there!" by pulling out my gun and asking him if I looked like the kind of a guy that got into lines, one should never flaunt firearms for such a petty reason. I could dream, though.

At the door, there were two guys standing guard, making sure no one jumped the gun and entered before the werewolves and chainsaw-wielding maniacs were in place. One guy, maybe a little younger than me, and who looked like he enjoyed the gym more than anything else in life, seemed to think about telling me about the line as well, but then he sized me up and realized I wouldn't be there for a few vicarious scares, and settled for raising a questioning eyebrow at me.

"I'm here to talk with Colton Yates."

"Don't know him," he answered.

The other guy, a middle-aged banker type, nodded. "He's one of the volunteers," he said, more for the gym bunny's benefit than for mine. "I think he's upstairs."

"I just need to talk with him for a minute," I said. Nobody moved. Suddenly it seemed like taking out the gun might not be such a bad idea after all. What were they afraid of, that I'd kidnap their zombie before showtime? Or that I was there to steal the secrets of their haunted house? I looked at Banker Guy, as he seemed the most reasonable. I tried my best smile, the one that gets me extra sprinkles on my cone at Ben & Jerry's. He relented, telling his partner to keep an eye on things and that he'd be right back. He then opened the front door, causing a huge cheer from the waiting crowd, which quickly changed to a disappointed moan when he closed it after we entered.

Inside, the mansion had truly been transformed. As I'd never been there, I couldn't be certain, but I was willing to bet the wooden railings that had been put in place to keep the ticket buyers going in a prescribed path weren't there year-round. Some rooms were blocked off entirely, while others were there for viewing purposes, with tableaux of Dracula rising from his coffin, a witch's cabin, complete with bubbling cauldron, and a mad scientist's laboratory, littered with brains in jars and bodies covered by bloody sheets, and so forth. I didn't see any actual spirits, but if the prickling on the back of my neck was anything to go by, and I knew it was, then the reputation of the house was warranted. I didn't blame the real ghosts from joining in on the festivities. They looked pretty lame.

My new friend took me down the hall and then through a little gate that had obviously been installed to keep the crowd from wandering where they shouldn't, and then we trudged up some stairs. At the first door on the left, he knocked.

"Yeah?" a female voice sounded.

"Someone here for Colton." Banker Guy, now that his chore was completed, nodded at me and departed. I opened the door.

Inside was a bedroom that was being used by the volunteers to get into their gory getups. A canopied bed dominated the room, but once you tore your eyes away from the god-awful yellow bed sheets, you noticed a nice fireplace, which unfortunately for the chilly room had no fire lit, several overstuffed chairs, and two little tables with mirrors. Both of the tables were occupied, one by Colton and the other by a young girl, maybe eighteen, although I'm a lousy guesser of age. Both of them were putting the finishing touches on their makeup, with Colton making sure his eyes looked sunken and the girl getting the blood dripping from her lips just right. She was a sparkly vampire. I wanted to shake her until she drooled. Vampires don't sparkle, no matter what modern movies tell people.

"You're late," Colton said, stating a fact. "I don't have much time. I've got to be down in the zombie room in just a few minutes."

"I didn't count on parking being such a bitch," I said. I looked at Sparkly. "Can you give us a few minutes alone?"

She checked herself one last time in the mirror. "I'm done anyway," she said. Her voice was high and squeaky. Maybe someone had already shaken her until she was loopy. That's what you get when you embrace the sparkly vampire mythology. She got up and grabbed her cape, which had been slung over the back of her chair. She put it on with a flourish, flashing me her plastic fangs. "How do I look?"

"Pale and hungry."

The girl grinned and strode to the door, telling Colton she'd see him later. Luckily, she didn't ask for details on my critique, as I'd have had to tell her she'd probably looked pale and hungry before donning her makeup, and now she looked stupid, pale, and hungry. Colton, on the other hand, didn't look bad, zombie-wise. Lots of nasty sores on the cheeks. Blackened teeth. I can't say he looked like any real zombie I'd ever met, but the crowd outside would be impressed. His eyes were tired, and makeup had nothing to do with that.

"You're going to see Matt and his band tonight?"

"Yeah." I went over to him and checked out his wrists and neck as he got his hair, thick with mousse, adjusted to his liking. No new marks anywhere I could see. Vamps don't always go for the neck, although it's the favored spot. Wrists are second. I won't even go into the third most popular, because it gives me phantom pains in my crotch just to think about it. "How are you feeling?"

"Tired," he admitted. "I slept all day too. Just couldn't get out of bed. And I'm still tired." He looked in the mirror and grimaced. "I nearly called off for tonight. It just seemed…. I don't know, a little stupid with everything going on. But I needed to keep my mind off things. Sitting around the house wasn't going to help anything."

He'd be spending the night surrounded by people, which was a good thing. "Have you heard from Matt?"

Colton shook his head. "No."

"Do you have somebody you can stay with tonight?" If everything went well, it wouldn't be necessary. Matt would be dust by the time Colton's zombie stint was over. But it never hurt to have an alternate plan.

"Yeah, I can probably arrange something." He turned to face me, his thin frame braced for the bad news he knew I was going to give him. With the zombie makeup in place, it was hard to read his expression, but he seemed to be doing well under the circumstances. "I have to know. Just what's going to happen tonight? What are you going to do?"

I wanted to lie and tell Colton I was just going to check the situation out, but I knew that wouldn't hold water. "I think you know."

His lip trembled. "You can't do that. There's got to be some other way."

"I'm sorry."

Colton closed his eyes tightly. "In the movies, sometimes if you kill the head vampire, the ones that he turned become human again."

"That's the movies." I put a hand on the kid's shoulder. "Matt is dead already. You've got to understand that."

Colton didn't reply at first. His face showed sorrow, which was quickly replaced by anger. He slammed his fist onto the table. I could tell it was me he wanted to hit. "You've got to do something! You can save him! I know you can!"

"I can't. No one can. I can just see that he's put to rest."

Colton stood suddenly. For a second I thought he was going to take a swing at me, and I think he did as well, but then he crumbled. He would have sunk to the floor if I hadn't reached out and grabbed him by the shoulders.

The tears began to flow in earnest. "I love him," he sobbed.

"I know. But this is what's best. Believe me."

Colton placed his head on my shoulder and let it all out, a real body-trembling cry that seemed to last hours but was actually no more than a few minutes. I waited until he was all cried out. "You okay?" I asked. Stupid question under the circumstances, but I had to say something.

Colton lifted his face and nodded. His chin trembled a bit, but he held it in. "What are you going to do?"

"What's walking around right now isn't your boyfriend." Not strictly true, but I didn't have time to go into the Vampire 101 course with Colton. In truth, the thing walking around inside Matt Hamilton's body was *mostly* Matt Hamilton, just a Matt Hamilton that was missing compassion and mercy. The lust for blood crushed out most other emotions. He'd kill his own granny for her Geritol-laden blood. "If I don't stop him, he'll kill quite a lot of people. Some of those people will become vampires themselves."

The young man before me was very still. "There's no other way?"

"The Matt you loved died days ago. I'm sorry."

"Maybe he's not—"

"He drank your blood. It's too late for him."

Colton wiped his eyes, smearing some of the zombie makeup. He didn't seem to care. We sat down and didn't speak for several minutes. Someone knocked on the door and yelled, "We're opening the doors in two minutes. I need everyone in places."

Colton turned to the mirror and made a few dabs at his eyes, fixing some of the damage. "I better go," he said, barely audibly.

He was trying to put on a brave face, but I knew there was no way he'd make it through the night. "You don't have to do this. I can take you someplace. To a friend's house."

He nodded briefly. "I'll need to tell Mr. Crannick."

"We'll tell him." Whoever Mr. Crannick was, he was going to be one zombie short tonight.

MOST of the crowd at the Lion's Den was younger than me by about a decade. It was a popular club in the area of town called Broadripple, known for its nightspots and music venues. The marquee outside had flashing lights and was advertising that The Scarlet Tide was playing that night in big, black letters. There was a bouncer at the door who was checking purses to make sure no one was carrying in drugs or firearms. When I came in, I thought he might frisk me, which would be unfortunate, as I not only had my gun in my holster but a wooden stake taped to my right leg just above my sock, and a silver dagger strapped to my left leg. The big silver cross hanging around my neck would have passed with no trouble, but he might have at least raised an eyebrow at the flask in my hip pocket. It contained holy water instead of whiskey, but for some reason he let me by without hesitation. I was glad, as I had no convincing story for my armaments other than that I was there to kill a vampire. And strangely, most people don't believe you when you tell them that.

Because of movies and books and even video games, there are a lot of misconceptions about vampires. On the other hand, a lot of it is true. Sunlight bugs the hell out of them, and if they are exposed to the sun's rays for too long, you get vampire flambé and no amount of sparkly sunblock will prevent it. A stake through the heart will kill them. Crosses work, but only if the vampire was religious—and Christian—when he was alive. I've always had the theory that their aversion to crucifixes is merely psychosomatic, but as far as I know, there haven't been any university studies to prove this. Same with holy water. Pisses me off when I douse a vamp with the stuff and it doesn't have any effect. Doesn't happen often, though. It seems that even if they weren't churchgoers when they were alive, if they even sort of think there's a God and that Jesus *might* have been his earthly son, the old standbys work. It's just when you get an atheist vampire that things go wonky. Vampires can't turn into bats or wolves or fluffy bunnies. And they smell. There's a musty, moldy scent to them. The only thing that seems to cover this smell is patchouli oil, so if you come across someone who reeks of patchouli, run away. They're either a vamp or an old hippie. Either way, safer to run.

Inside the Lion's Den, I couldn't smell any patchouli. Mostly sweat and beer. The place was packed, and I had to work my way through the crowd to get close enough to the stage to get a gander at the band, which was already well into the set. The music was loud, and I could feel the drum beat jarring my bones. At a reasonable sound level, I might have enjoyed them. Doubtful, but anything was possible. As it was, all I could make out were shouts into the microphone and instruments that seemed to blast into my brain.

Wow. I really was getting old.

The band looked much the same as they did on the flier. All in black. Dark eyes made darker with eye shadow. They all had tattoos, some more than others. The lead singer seemed to be the girl. She was redheaded and festooned with ink and piercings. I concentrated on the bass player, the tall, lanky Matt Hamilton. He was wearing a sleeveless black shirt, maybe to show off the tattoo on his right bicep. It was hard to make out what it depicted from where I was standing, but at a guess, I'd say it showed a devil devouring a naked woman. I preferred Wile E. Coyote.

Looking at him up on the stage, you wouldn't know he'd become a bloodsucker. A mediocre bass player, maybe, but a vampire, no. He was pale, true, but hell, they all were. Every now and then he'd step up to his microphone and sing a line, backing up the lead singer. He had a thin, reedy voice. He looked like a nice young man. I wondered how many people he'd killed since he'd become a vampire.

I briefly took in the drummer, a small guy with limp light-brown hair that hung down over his face. Every now and then he'd throw his head back to get the strands out of his eyes. They'd only fall forward again seconds later, causing a vicious cycle.

And then there was the lead guitarist. His shoulder-length brown hair had some body to it, so he didn't have the same problems as the drummer. He had his head down, concentrating on his playing, so at first I couldn't see his face. Once his solo was over and the female singer began blasting out another verse, he raised his face, and I could see him properly for the first time. The crowd hooted with approval over his solo, and a twitch of a smile played upon his lips. He had a wide mouth and prominent cheekbones and deep-set eyes. At first I thought he wasn't very attractive, but then some girl in the audience shouted something at him. I couldn't make out what she said, as she was battling a loud sound system, but the guitarist must have made it out, because he broke into a full grin that lit up his face. It changed my mind about him, and I found myself thinking, "I'd do him." Hey, just because you're on a diet, doesn't mean you can't look at the menu.

I listened halfheartedly to the rest of the song, which seemed to go on for an eternity. I tried to keep my eyes on Hamilton, but I kept finding myself checking out the lead guitarist. The guy certainly didn't have classic good looks, but he exuded sex appeal. Maybe it was the guitar. Guitars make you sexy. Look at Keith Richards. I've seen zombies better looking than that dude, and he hasn't had any trouble attracting mates. I'm sure the truckloads of money he has doesn't hurt.

When the song ended, I felt a stirring in my pants, which had nothing to do with sexy guitar players. I'd set my phone on vibrate, knowing I'd never hear a ring inside the Lion's Den. I checked to see who was calling. Nick.

I replaced my phone in my pocket and started to force my way to the exit as the next song started. I had plenty of time. Matt wasn't going to chomp anyone's neck during their set, so I could step outside for a while and chat with Nick without worry. Besides, my bones needed a rest from the sonic bombardment they were getting.

I got my hand stamped and went outside. It had begun to rain a little, just enough to wet the sidewalks. There were a few smokers hunkering against the building trying to get in a quick nicotine fix before heading back in for more music. I moved away from them and called Nick.

"Yeah?" I said.

"You've got to help me," he said. "I had no idea it would be this bad."

I'd been waiting for his call, and I had to swallow saying "I told you so" in both English and Latin. Not that I knew the Latin phrase, but I was sure I could find it somewhere on the Internet. I looked about me. Drops of rain were coming off the plant in the decorative tub I was standing near, soaking my shoes. I moved away a few paces, still making sure I was out of earshot of the smokers or anyone strolling down the sidewalk. "Keep calm," I told him.

Calm wasn't possible at the moment. "I saw an old lady in the parking lot at Kroger's earlier, after I'd gotten my groceries. I thought she was just a regular old lady. Granted, I did think it was odd that she was wearing just a thin dress and I was shivering in my jacket, but…." He ran out of words. He regrouped. "She just looked at me and then vanished."

"They do that."

"And there was a kid, a teenager. He was walking down the street, looking so lost. I didn't even think much about it. Just another kid, you know? And then he turned around. His face was half blown away!"

"Nick, I—"

"I tried to talk to him. I figured that's why I asked Gina to do this, so I'd better just suck it up and talk to the kid. So I told him my name and that I wanted to help him. He just stares at me and then he disappears, too! I mean… what the fuck!"

"Are you upset because you saw them, or because you couldn't help them?"

There was a brief silence as he thought about that. When he replied, his voice had lost some of its desperation. "Both. I mean, I really wanted to help them. I was scared, I don't mind telling you. I guess I just didn't think I'd find ghosts just… out. Out walking around. Somehow, I just thought they'd be in houses, haunting away.

And I really didn't think that they might look… well, damaged. That poor kid. His jaw was nearly gone. I think he must have shot himself. Robbie died in a car wreck and he doesn't look like a crash-test dummy. Why did this kid—?" He ran out of words again.

"Some of them look as they did in life, some look like they did when they died. I don't know why. Some of them can appear in different forms, even as themselves at a different age." Robbie couldn't, as we'd learned over the years. Neither of us knew why. Even me, the go-to answer guy when it came to ghosts, didn't have all the answers. "You have to understand, Nick, that most people don't even linger. They go to the other side right away. Some stay behind a day or two. On rare occasions, they stay longer. Robbie is one of the rare ones. And it seems like the longer they stay, the more control they have over their appearance and how they can communicate with the living. The ones you saw, probably, were new spirits. They didn't know how to talk with you, so they vanished. You may have scared them just as much as they scared you."

"But if I can't talk to them, if I can't help them, then what the hell did I do this for?"

"I tried to talk you out of it, but you wouldn't listen."

"I just wanted to help," Nick said weakly.

"And you will. There are spirits out there that will be ready to talk with you. You just have to find them, or let them find you."

I heard him take a deep breath. I had been lost in the conversation, and didn't notice I'd been pacing and was now back against the potted plant, and I was close enough that the wet leaves were making a dark spot on my jeans, midthigh. I moved away from the plant. It had stopped raining, except for a few overzealous drops. The smokers had started to emerge from the eaves and overhangs, and were getting louder. I cupped a hand around the phone so I could hear Nick better.

"Thanks for listening," he said. "I think I'm okay now. Just had a little panic moment there." Another deep breath. "So what are you doing tonight?"

"Staking a vampire, then not much." One of the smokers had wandered closer and her eyes grew wide when she heard me. Or maybe she just saw the wet spot on my jeans and thought I'd peed myself. I moved further away from her. "Probably watch some more *Star Trek* later. You can join me, if you like."

"School night," he replied. "Some of us have to keep somewhat regular hours. Staking a vampire? Isn't that hard to do during the night, while they're up and around?"

"Hey, if Buffy and Abraham Lincoln can do it, so can I," I said. Actually, Nick was right, and normally I just tracked them to their lair and poked them with a stick while they slumbered, but this one was living with my client, and I didn't think he wanted to see me kill his boyfriend in their bedroom. "Speaking of vamps, I really should be getting back to it. They don't stake themselves, you know. Call me if you need me, though."

"I'm heading to bed, so unless they come and jostle me in my sleep, I think I'm safe."

We said our good-byes and hung up. I hadn't noticed, but the female smoker had edged closer and probably had overheard the rest of my chat with Nick. She was looking at me as if trying to decide if she should call the men in the white coats to come and get me, the cops, or just start screaming. Or maybe I was a harmless lunatic. I grinned at her as I walked back down the sidewalk to the club. As I passed her, I said, "I've got a dog that's a zombie."

"Okay," she said, drawing the word out. I was in the harmless lunatic category now, and she would have a story to tell her friends.

Back inside, the band was still shaking the rafters. I got as close to the stage as I could and pretended I was enjoying the songs. Finally, they finished their set and walked off the stage. The crowd hooted and hollered and they came back on. The lead guitarist leaned into his microphone.

"We've got one more for you," he said, his voice deep and guttural. They started to play, but I was already moving, working my way to the exit. My Plan A was to catch Hamilton going out the stage door, and follow him to some nice spot where I could kill him.

Plan B was a dream. In Plan B, he came out on his own and there was just him and me in the alley, and I could finish up quickly and maybe get home in time to catch *The Daily Show.*

I was familiar enough with the Lion's Den to know the stage door lead out to the alley between the club and the coffee shop next door. There were apartments above the coffee shop, and the building had one of those rickety fire escapes. The fire escape made a nice shadowy area away for me to stand and wait. There were no groupies waiting by the stage door wanting to get autographs from The Scarlet Tide. I guess they weren't that popular yet. I leaned against the wall and kept my eye on the door. If I'd been Sam Spade, I would have smoked half a pack of cigarettes while waiting, the butts piling up on the damp asphalt around me. I wasn't Sam Spade. But then, Sam didn't have a dead boyfriend still hanging around. I figured I came out better on that deal, as ghosts didn't give you cancer. It was odd what your mind came up with as you were standing in an alley waiting for a vampire to emerge.

I'd gone over my grocery list, thought about joining a gym, and was humming a Tom Petty tune when a screech of metal brought me out of my thoughts. The stage door of the Lion's Den was opening.

The light from within seemed abnormally bright until my eyes adjusted. I heard sounds spilling out into the alley. Laughter, and a deep male voice saying, "See you later, buddy." Then there was a shadow in the doorway, followed by a tall, willowy figure wearing a leather jacket.

I couldn't believe my luck. It was Matt Hamilton, and he was alone. He closed the door behind him and stood for a moment, moving his head around to work the kinks out of his neck. Even from where I was, I could smell the patchouli. As soon as the door opened, I'd prepared myself, retrieving the stake from around my leg. I slipped it under my armpit and got out my flask and twisted off the cap. Now I was ready. Left hand, stake. Right hand, holy water. Plan: douse vamp's face with holy water, and while he's burning and screaming, ram stake into his heart. Easy peasy lemon squeezy. At least in theory. The trouble with theories was that they could go to shit in an instant.

It would have been lovely to follow the bastard and sneak up on him and stake him from behind, but vampires have really good night vision, and Matt Hamilton spotted me even though I was in the deep shadows. I didn't think he saw the flask or stake, because he didn't even give a flicker of worry. In fact, he licked his lips.

"Well," he said, "who have we here?"

"Fan of yours," I said. I tensed my muscles, ready to spring.

I was expecting him to spot the vamp-killing paraphernalia and scamper, and I was gearing up for a long chase. He moved quickly, but not down the alley. He charged right at me, snarling. I tried to dodge, but I wasn't quick enough. Maybe that gym idea deserved a second look. In an instant, he was on me, pinning me against the wall. His right hand grasped my throat with strength I was sure he hadn't possessed when he'd been alive. It was like a vise gripping my windpipe. His eyes seemed to glow red in the dim light and he opened his mouth wide, revealing his fangs. His hand twisted my head so that he could get a good chomp on my neck.

I shot my right hand up, splashing some of the holy water right in his face. The effect was instantaneous. Smoke curled up from the spots where the liquid had hit, and there was a sizzling sound that reminded me of burgers on the grill. Note to self—don't go out vamp killing on an empty stomach. Thinking of Burger King while a vampire has you by the throat can get you killed.

Hamilton shrank back, releasing my throat. He screamed in pain and bent over nearly double, clutching at his face. Between his fingers, I could see some sores that had erupted on his face, angry red blotches caused by contact with the holy juice. Good stuff. I'm not Catholic myself, but I'm glad they're around. They have neat toys.

A sound escaped my throat as air was once again allowed to travel to my lungs. That was my only hesitation, and before Hamilton even straightened, I rushed forward and jabbed the stake as hard as I could into his back.

I'm pretty strong, but try shoving a wooden stake into somebody's back and getting it to pierce his heart. Not easy, even with the pointiest of points on your stake. I buried the sucker pretty far in, but perhaps not quite enough, because he let out a roar and stood erect. Blind with rage, he swung both arms out with all of his strength. His right hit me on the upper chest, and I flew back. I hit a dumpster and would have collapsed onto the ground, but Hamilton rushed forward and grabbed me by the collar of my jacket. We struggled for a moment, his fangs uncomfortably close to my neck. I caught a glimpse of the stake, still in his back. The wound was gushing blood, and as we wrestled around, I got a lot of it on me. My dry cleaner was going to have a fit over the mess. Hamilton continued to yell in pain, and I was vaguely aware of shouts and people talking from somewhere close by. Hard to really care about the rest of the world, though, when a vampire's teeth are inches from your neck.

"Fuck this shit," I said as I shoved Hamilton as hard as I could. He fell back and hit the opposite wall with enough force that the stake was driven further into his body. Enough to do the trick, anyway. In fact, I caught sight of the tip of the stake bursting through his chest and the gleam of blood spurting out before he slumped to the ground and shadows hid the gore. It was so fast, I wasn't sure I actually saw the stake push all the way through his thin body, or if I just imagined it. Maybe it was wishful thinking. The bastard's grip on my neck would probably leave bruises, so I wanted to see the spilling of some vamp blood.

He had fallen a little to the side, back still against the wall and his feet straight out. The casual passerby might mistake him for one of Indianapolis's homeless souls who had consumed a little too much Ripple and was sleeping it off. I knew he was dead. Well, dead again. His face was lowered, but I could see he looked peaceful. The bloodlust was gone. So was everything else.

I took a few steps toward him, rubbing my throat. I stopped when I heard someone clapping their hands in applause. I turned, the movement making me realize I was still a little woozy from Hamilton's strangulation.

The Scarlet Tide

Standing by the stage door were three people, all dressed in black. The rest of the members of The Scarlet Tide had come out, but they weren't screaming or shouting for the cops. The lead guitarist was standing slightly in front of the singer and the drummer, and it had been his hands doing the clapping. There was the hint of a smile on his lips. The other two were stone faced.

"Do you know," the guitarist asked, "how hard it is to find a good bass player in this town?"

The other two moved, the girl to the left and the guy to the right, cutting off the alley. I looked quickly behind me. The other end of the alley was barred by a high wire fence. I was trapped.

And in deep shit, because the other members of The Scarlet Tide were vampires too.

CHAPTER 5

YOU know that sinking feeling you get when you realize the rope hoisting the piano up to the fourth floor has snapped and you're standing directly under it, and you think, "Oh, this is going to hurt"? Neither do I, but I imagine it has nothing on the feeling you get when you're surrounded in an alley by a bunch of vamps who just watched you kill one of their buddies.

The guitarist took a few steps forward. He was relaxed and casual, which made sense. He wasn't the one about to become a Happy Meal to a trio of bloodsuckers. His smile grew. "Now, that wasn't a very nice thing to do, was it?"

I backpedaled a little, hoping it didn't look like I was scared and trying to keep my distance from him. I was, but one wants to look cool, if at all possible. "We didn't see eye to eye on some things. He wanted to drink my blood. I wanted to shove a stake through his heart."

Holy crap, the guy's smile grew even wider. He had a huge grin, reminding me of the Joker in the *Batman* movies. "Well, I wouldn't want us not to see eye to eye. Let's introduce ourselves. I'd like to know who killed Matt. I was beginning to like him, and he wasn't a bad bass player."

He'd stopped moving, so I did too. I tried to find something out of the corner of my eye, something I could use as a weapon or as a means of escape. Nothing popped out. I raised an eyebrow at the guy. "You want to know my name?"

He shrugged. "It helps to know where to send the remains. Not that there will be much."

I didn't feel like being one-upped by one of the walking dead. "You first."

"My," he said after barking out a laugh, "you've got *cojones*, don't you?" When I didn't reply or move, he shrugged again. "Why not?" He tilted his head toward the drummer without taking his eyes off me. "Tell him your names."

The blonde kid looked like he'd rather eat raw sewage than be pleasant to me, but he obeyed. "I'm Braedon. Braedon Isaacs."

The girl with the tattoos spoke up. "Kissy Peters."

"I'm sorry?" I said.

"Kissy Peters," she repeated, spitting out the words.

I'd always wondered how James Bond kept a straight face when the villainess of the piece told him her name was Pussy Galore or some such nonsense. Granted, the threat of imminent death makes it hard to let the guffaws fly indiscriminately, but on the other hand, if you're going to die anyway, you want to annoy your killers in any way possible. "That's what's on your birth certificate?"

She glared at me. I don't think she found me humorous.

"And I'm Dominic," the one closest to me said. "Dominic Hunt."

I nodded. "Nice to meet you."

"And you are?" he asked.

"Getting out of here," I said as I rushed forward.

I yanked the thin chain holding the cross around my neck until it broke. With the cross in my right hand, I covered the ground between me and Hunt before he realized what was happening. I dodged to his left side, thinking if I got past him, I had a better chance with the ridiculously named Kissy than the drummer.

Hunt reached out to grab me, but I shoved the cross into his face before he could get his mitts on me. The silver made contact with his forehead, and I heard the satisfying hiss as his skin blistered. Good. He had been at least semireligious in life. I had the sense that he was a much older vamp than the rest of them, which made him more likely to be affected by religious icons. He let out a howl and clutched his brow with one hand while lashing out with his other.

Unfortunately for him, I was already out of his reach and barreling into tattoo girl. Kissy saw me coming and was braced for impact, her fangs bared, but I hit her lower than she expected. I ducked my head and hit her in the lower abdomen. We both tumbled, and as we went down, my left shoulder hit the brick wall hard enough to send a jolt of pain through my whole body, but somehow I managed to keep hold of the cross.

Kissy's head fared worse, thudding against the wall. It would have knocked out a human. Vamps are made of sterner stuff, though. It just pissed her off. We ended up tangled in a heap, with me half on top of her. I tried to scramble off, but she grabbed hold of my jacket and tried to pull me closer to her face so her fangs could find their mark.

I managed to press the cross against the arm holding my jacket. There came the lovely hiss as her skin boiled, and a thin stream of smoke drifted up from the wound. Not a lot, though. In life, she must have been only semireligious. She didn't let go entirely, but I got enough leverage room to get my knees under me. She didn't seem to want to give up the fight, so I reared back and smacked the cross against the side of her head. That did it. Even semireligious types will feel a whack on the side of the head.

Before I could get to my feet, I felt hands gripping the back of my neck. Braedon hadn't been idle, and was joining the fray. And while he was a smaller guy, the vamp strength made him dangerous. He growled and tossed me aside. It wasn't a gentle toss. I'm pretty sure I was airborne for a second or two before I hit the pavement. I rolled, hoping to lessen the impact as much as possible. I don't know if that was successful or not, because I felt like I'd been pummeled by Muhammad Ali in his prime.

I quickly saw, though, that drummer Braedon had done me a favor. Instead of tossing me further into the alley, where I'd have still been trapped like a rat in a maze, he'd thrown me closer to the entrance to the alley. So close, in fact, that the light from one of the nearby streetlamps was hitting me. I pushed aside the pain and scrambled to my feet. I heard him giving chase, but I had a good head start. Springing to my feet, I bolted toward the street. Adrenaline can do marvels when you're being chased by a vampire.

I knew I didn't have much left in me, but I tore out of the alley and went left. There were more lights that way, flashing ones. Blue flashing ones. And a bright spotlight that made it hard to see the cop several yards in front of me with his gun drawn. Someone had heard the ruckus in the alleyway and dialed 911.

"Hold it right there!" he shouted.

I stopped. My legs felt like rubber anyway. I wanted to give them a special medal for getting me this far. Another cop—at least I assumed it was a man in blue—off to my side yelled, "Freeze! Hands in the air!"

Part of my mind was aware the footsteps behind me had disappeared, meaning that either vamp Braedon had also stopped in his tracks or, more likely, had skedaddled back into the alley. Most of my mind, though, was concentrating on the fact that there were at least two guns aimed at me.

I'd never been so glad to be accosted by the police in my life.

I WAS slumped in a chair across Lieutenant David Carson's desk when he sauntered into his office toting a thin file. It was morning, and I hadn't slept. He didn't look like he had either. His suit was in need of a pressing and there were dark circles under his eyes. He maneuvered around the desk, not looking at me, his shoulders slumped. Sinking into his chair, he sighed as if all the world's troubles had been dumped on him.

Before speaking, he gazed at the ceiling as if asking God for patience to deal with me. "Several patrons at the Lion's Den reported a fracas in the alley—"

"They used that word? Fracas?" I asked.

Carson ignored the interruption. "And who do we find running out of the alley? My favorite private investigator, Duncan Andrews.

In the alley, my men find a body with a wooden stake through its heart."

"People just leave their litter anywhere nowadays."

The veins in Carson's neck started doing a little dance. I think he counted to ten before speaking again. If so, it didn't really calm him down much. "Dammit, Andrews, you've really gone and done it this time! You're found fleeing the scene of a homicide—"

"Is it homicide if the guy's already dead?"

Carson started to shout something else at me, swallowed his words with difficulty, and instead rubbed the back of his neck. When that didn't seem to help, he sighed another deep one. "Yeah, that's another thing. The preliminary medical report shows the guy had been dead for about a week."

"But yet he played a mean bass guitar at the Lion's Den last night."

Shaking his head, Carson muttered, "Just one time, I'd like to find you on a scene where I don't end up with weird shit happening all around me. Tell me what the hell's going on."

"Off the record?"

He stared at me. "I've never been able to put anything you do *on* the record, at least not without obscuring half of what really was going on. What the hell is it this time?"

"Stake in the heart. I'm sure you can figure it out."

Carson's face showed disbelief. "Vampires? You expect me to believe that Count Dracula is running around Indianapolis, biting people on the neck and sucking their blood?"

"When have I ever lied to you?" I asked with what I hoped was a hopeful smile.

"Hundreds of times!" Carson leaned back in his chair and bit a thumbnail. It must have been pretty tasty, because he gave that sucker quite a chewing. Finished, he glared at me. "Vampires?"

"Fangs and all."

He found another nail to chew. It seemed to relax him. "I've heard you say some cockamamie things in my time—"

"Cockamamie. Can I just say I'm loving your vocabulary today?"

I was too tired to care much about the angry glare he shot me. "Vampires. Now I've heard everything." He shook his head. "I should have locked you up years ago. You've been nothing but trouble since I met you." He pushed at the file he'd laid on his desk. "You see the problem I have? I have a dead body with a stake in its heart. There were hundreds of witnesses that could testify that this same dead body was up and walking around just hours before getting the stake in his heart. I also have a report stating that this Hamilton guy had been dead for over a week! Hell, right now I'm in favor of locking myself up so I don't have to deal with this!"

I waited. I wasn't getting the vibe from Carson that he was ready to toss me in a cell and throw away the key. Instead I had the feeling he was buying what I was saying, at least in part, and was trying to figure out how to spin the tale into something that would make sense on a police report.

Carson had been with me on too many strange cases. He knew, although I didn't think he liked to admit it, that there were creatures out there best left in the shadows. Creatures the police weren't capable of handling. Carson had seen a lot of things. A guy getting nibbled to death by squirrels. A zombie trying to eat some dude's brains in the parking lot outside of Kohl's. You can't witness that kind of thing firsthand and just dismiss it outright. You can officially refuse to accept it, but in his heart, Carson knew the score.

Another sigh. "Your statement," he said in a flat tone, "says that you came across the body in the alley and were in pursuit of another person, who you thought might have been the killer."

"It sounded good at the time."

Carson snorted. "And the officers who arrived at the scene mysteriously didn't see this supposed killer."

"He was really, really fast."

Raising an eyebrow, Carson asked, "What really happened?"

"I killed one vamp and was being chased by another." I gave Carson the *Reader's Digest Condensed* version of the night's events, ending with, "I thought it best to leave most of that out of my statement."

"I can see where you might," Carson said glumly. He rubbed a hand across his nose and gave a tired snort. "I'm not sure I'm ready to accept vampires."

"I'm willing to listen to other explanations. You tell me how a dead man can play two sets to a packed house and nearly throttle me to death."

"I can't. But… vampires!"

"A band of vampires, in several senses. When you think of it, it's a good profession for the undead. They can play to crowds at night and then feed off groupies. They like the nightlife, they like to boogie."

Carson picked up a pencil. I thought for a second he was going to throw it at me, and I think for a moment he did too, but he merely twiddled it in his fingers. "If I accept that I've got vampires running around the city—and, mind you, I'm not saying I'm ready for that— but if I accept that, I've got a few questions for you, since you seem to be the expert in all things weird."

"Shoot."

"Am I going to have a vampire epidemic on my hands? I mean, the people they bite become vampires too, don't they? Isn't this going to spread like the plague?"

"The victims only become vampires if they die from the vampire's bite. And that doesn't generally happen. Vampires tend to feed off different people each night, and then they don't drain the victims. And a lot of the ones that do become vampires don't live long. They make mistakes. There's no vampire manual that tells them what to avoid, so unless another vamp takes them under his wing—sorry about the pun—they tend to do stupid things like crawl out of their graves during the day. That fries them. Or they try to live their normal lives, sleeping in a bed with the curtains tightly drawn, but then some unknowing soul comes in and says, 'Hey, it's too dark in here. Let's let in some sunlight!' and voomp! Toasted vamp."

Carson tapped the pencil against the desktop. He bit his lip, then said, "I can certainly see if we can find the other members of this band. I'd want to question them in any case. How the hell I'm going to keep this from getting in the papers, I have no idea. A corpse playing in a band!" He shook his head. I almost felt sorry for him. He consulted his file. "Braedon Isaacs, Jennifer Peters, and Dominic Hunt."

"Your men can't deal with them. They're dangerous."

"We'll see if we can get addresses for them and go from there."

"Jennifer Peters, huh? She told me her name was Kissy."

Did I see the trace of a smirk cross Carson's face? "Kissy is her stage name, apparently. I got that much from the owner of the club."

"Get anything else from him?"

Carson shrugged. "He didn't seem to know a lot about the group. Tonight was their first show there. He's expecting them back tonight, though. They've got another gig there tonight, and they left all their equipment."

"They won't be back for it. They know their secret is out."

Carson shoved the file aside and went back to tapping his pencil. "If you're right—"

"And I am."

"Then I'd appreciate it if you'd take care of the situation as quickly as possible. I'll cut you as much slack as I possibly can. I don't want anyone else getting hurt. And since you're the go-to guy when there's anything spooky going on...." He frowned. "Indianapolis isn't on a Hellmouth or anything like that, is it? Is that why all this weird stuff happens here?"

"Why, Lieutenant, you've been watching TV!" I grinned. "Been catching up on reruns of *Buffy the Vampire Slayer?* But to answer your question, no. Indianapolis is not on a Hellmouth. But good try."

"That's good." He looked relieved.

"The Hellmouth is up in Carmel. The vamps and demons just prefer the city to the suburbs."

That got me a glare, as he couldn't tell if I was kidding or not.

CHAPTER 6

"HE'S dead," Colton said numbly. "Matt's dead."

I shifted uncomfortably. "Yeah. I'm very sorry."

He nodded, seeming to take in my words without them really registering. His eyes were filling with tears, although none were falling as of yet. He was attempting to hold back the deluge. "That's it, then," he said.

He'd asked me for details. I told him what happened in the alley. I didn't go into detail. Colton didn't need to hear that. I made it sound simple. I wondered if I should go on, explaining that every member of Matt's band had been a vamp, but I could tell by Colton's glassy eyes that he'd stopped listening. "So he died in an alley?"

"The vampire died in an alley. Matt really died several days ago, probably shortly after he ran out on you. He was already dead. I just killed the vampire."

"In an alley." His voice sounded hollow.

"The official word is going to be that he was killed by a mugger."

Colton swallowed hard. "I must owe you some money," he said, getting up off the ratty couch. Once Carson had let me go my merry little way, I headed straight for Colton's place to break the news to him. I owed him that much. The small apartment was clean but furnished in what looked like hand-me-downs or stuff they'd found at garage sales. He moved to the kitchen counter to retrieve his checkbook.

"There's no charge," I said. I tried to say something more, something comforting, but the words didn't come to me.

With slumped shoulders, he stood in the tiny kitchenette with one hand on the counter. The true weight of his boyfriend's death was just hitting him. The tears started to roll down his cheeks. He turned slightly, not wanting me to see. I rose, feeling stupid and lame and useless.

"Lieutenant Carson from the Indianapolis PD will be getting in touch with you," I said. I'm not sure he heard me. Colton cried silently for a few moments, and then rushed past me to a door down the short hallway, which I assumed was the bedroom. He slammed the door behind him.

I let myself out, thinking of what I'd done to that kid. Granted, I could hardly have allowed his boyfriend to keep on sucking the life out of Colton, but I wouldn't be getting a fee and I'd made a mess out of Colton Yates's life. Good going, Andrews.

"SO," ROBBIE said, "you're in one of those moods."

I was sitting on the couch at our place, Daisy snuggled up next to me. The TV was on and I'd been gazing at it without really paying attention to it. "One of what moods?"

He was perched on the arm of a chair, wearing nothing but a pair of black basketball shorts. For a moment, I shifted from the TV to him, thinking how hot nearly anyone looked in basketball shorts, but Robbie especially. Then I remembered it didn't matter how hot Robbie looked. I couldn't touch him, at least not in the way I wanted, so my eyes went back to the TV. The huge, hunky frame of Jared Padalecki filled the screen. I couldn't touch him either. I continued to pet Daisy. She sighed contentedly. At least one of us was happy.

"One of those 'I hate myself' moods." Robbie smiled at me, attempting encouragement. "Want to talk about it?"

I shook my head. "No." Unconsciously, I'd stopped petting Daisy. She raised her head as if to say "what the fuck," so I scratched her between the ears some. She narrowed her bloodshot eyes, enjoying the feeling. I watched *Supernatural* for a few minutes, then said, "I just hate it when I have a case and it's a no-win situation. I had a client whose boyfriend was a vampire. I killed him. Now my client's a wreck. But what choice did I have? It's not like I could have helped the guy. Once you're a vamp, you're sunk. There's no way back. Not even Gina could have made him human again. Dead is dead. And why don't vamps turn into dust like they do on TV? No muss, no fuss. I wouldn't have had to spend all night in a police station if there hadn't been a body lying in an alley with a stake through the heart. And now I know there are at least three vampires running around town, and I know I'll search for them and destroy them and I won't make a cent from it. I hate to sound petty, but this is supposed to be a business. If I keep on killing the boogeyman for free, soon I won't be able to eat. But if I don't take care of the situation, who will?"

Robbie nodded sagely. "Well, since you don't want to talk about it—"

"I just wish there had been something else I could have done. Some way to make the situation right. But it was too late for Matt Hamilton. He'd technically been dead for several days. One of the other members of his group must have turned him. I bet it was that lead guitarist guy. That Dominic. He looks like the type that enjoys draining a body and killing someone."

"It seems like—"

"And then I broke the news to his boyfriend," I went on, interrupting Robbie. "I didn't have to do that. I could have let Carson give him the news. He would have then called me in a day or two and told me there was no case, as his boyfriend was dead, and that would have been it. But no! I had to be the one to tell him that he'd never see his boyfriend alive again."

"Well, you did the right thing. He needed to know."

Daisy huffed a little. I had stopped scratching. I went back to petting her. The dog and I sighed simultaneously. "You should have seen him, Robbie. It was like I'd knocked the life right out of him. It'll take ages for him to recover from this."

Robbie moved off the arm of the chair and came over and sat down next to me, with Daisy in between us. He put his arm around my shoulder. I couldn't really feel the contact, just a chill around my neck. "You did what you could. You did what you had to do."

We sat there for a while, not talking. *Supernatural* had ended. Some other show came on. I wasn't sure what it was, but what little I saw of it looked like crap. There was a cute guy on it, but he couldn't act worth shit. The director must have realized this and used every excuse to have the guy take his shirt off, which was a little consolation, but not much. Finally, I picked up the remote and switched off the set.

I looked at Robbie. "When you look at me, what do you see?"

He frowned. "What the heck do you mean by that? I see you, of course."

"I'm getting some gray hair, especially at the temples."

"Been meaning to mention that to you. It looks kind of sexy, if you ask me."

"And crow's feet. I'm getting lines on my face."

"You're approaching middle age. It happens."

"It won't happen to you."

He looked at me, his face serious. One thing I always liked about Robbie, he knew when I wanted him to knock off the kidding. "No, it won't."

"What are we going to do about that?"

Robbie gave that some thought, scrunching his mouth around as he worked on what to say. Finally, he shook his head. "I don't know."

"It just seems like…. I don't know… like our time is running out."

He frowned at me. "Do you want me to move on?"

Robbie had tried to move on before, but I'd talked him out of it. I wasn't ready to have him out of my life, difficult as our relationship was. I shook my head. "No, I don't want that."

"What then?"

I looked down, not wanting to see his face when he heard my words. "I want you to be alive."

He didn't reply. There was nothing he could have said anyway. I picked the remote back up and turned the TV on again. The horrible actor had his shirt off and was fighting with another bad actor, who was also shirtless. The program was showing some improvement.

I WAS having a productive morning, of sorts. I'd first given myself a slight case of McIndigestion from wolfing down a fast-food breakfast in record time, and then visited my bank to deposit a check that had been sitting on my desk for two weeks. While I was there, I had the teller look to see if some kind stranger had deposited a million dollars into my account. They hadn't. As I walked back to where I'd parked my car on New York Street, I called Gina on my cell phone. Like me, she isn't normally an early riser, so I was somewhat surprised when she actually answered.

"How's the hometown?" I asked.

"I haven't decided yet" was her reply. "It's changed a lot since I was here last."

"A couple hundred years will do that to a town."

"They certainly have embraced their witchy heritage. There's a psychic fair going on, tours, and more women in pointy hats than you can shake a stick at. Today we're going to the Turner-Ingersoll Mansion."

"Oh," I said, hoping I sounded interested.

She laughed. "You'd know it better as the House of the Seven Gables."

"Ah. Well, hopefully the house is better than the book. I think Hawthorne induces snoring."

"Philistine. He was a nice man. A little stuffy, but nice. What's happening your way?"

"Not much. Vampires in town, so I'll be killing them. You know, the usual."

"Never a dull moment. Be careful. They have pointy teeth."

"I had noticed that. Have you broken the news to Mark yet? That he's dating a much, much older woman?"

"Oh hell, I'm just going to tell him I'm a witch. We won't go into the age thing until later. I don't want to freak him out."

"Because, of course, he won't freak out when he finds out you're a witch."

"We'll find out tonight. I'll let you know how it goes. I'd better go now. Mark's just come out of the bathroom, so I guess we're ready to head out. If I see Nathaniel Hawthorne's ghost today, I'll tell him you think he's a shitty author."

"Please do. Give Mark my love."

We rang off. I was just turning the corner by the *Indianapolis Star* building when my phone chirped. I thought it would be Gina again, having forgotten to tell me something, but it was Nick. He sounded horrible.

"Can you come by? I need to talk."

"Be right over. You're at the school?"

"Home. I called in sick." He laughed hollowly. "Not far from the truth."

I got to my car and found that I'd spent too long in line at the bank for the amount of coins I'd put in the parking meter. There was a ticket sticking up out of the windshield wipers. Great. Another depletion in the bank balance. I got into the car and tossed the ticket in the glove box. Out of sight, out of mind. I'd deal with it later. Somehow, with Nick freaking out, me worrying about getting older with a boyfriend who would never age, and vampires prancing around town biting people willy-nilly, a parking ticket didn't seem that important.

I made good time getting to the west side of town and Nick's place. I was greeted at the door by Nick and his two cats. Jasmine and Winter looked happy and well-fed. Nick didn't. His dark hair hadn't seen shampoo for a day or two and was sticking up in odd-looking tufts, and his eyes were so bloodshot they'd give Daisy's a run for their money, which wasn't a good thing, as Daisy was technically dead. Nick also hadn't shaved, but the stubble wasn't a bad look on him. He was wearing black sweatpants and a worn blue T-shirt that looked like he'd slept in them.

He ushered me in with words that came out as an unintelligible grumble. Jasmine wove her lithe body around my legs as I walked into the living room and picked out a spot on the couch. Winter was less effusive in his greeting, watching me from the doorway as if saying, "Yeah, I know you, but I'm trying to decide if you deserve to pet me or not." With a twitch of his nose, he sauntered over to an armchair and hopped up. He did that cat thing where he kept an eye on me but was trying to look like he *wasn't* keeping an eye on me.

Nick chose a chair opposite the cat. Before he sat down, he sniffed the air, and then his armpit. "I stink," he said. "Haven't taken a shower yet."

"I've smelled worse."

"I've been up all night."

"So I gathered. Want to tell me about it?"

Nick tried sitting up, but that seemed to take too much effort, so he threw his head back and became one with the chair. "I think a ghost followed me home last night."

"They do that every now and then. Especially when they realize you can see them." In my younger days, it had happened often. Nowadays, not so much. Maybe now I just didn't exude that I-want-to-help-you vibe. Maybe it was the fact that I often carried a gun, although why a gun should worry a ghost is beyond me. It's not as if I could kill them again.

Nodding, Nick went on. "I wasn't even really sure anything was going on until I went to bed, although I kept getting the feeling all night that I was being watched. As soon as I turned off the lights, I saw this shadow appear at the base of my bed. A few seconds later, the shadow became a young man. Duncan, I don't think I've ever seen anyone with so much sorrow in their face."

Jasmine jumped up on my legs and looked up at me. She gave out a tiny meow, and I took the hint and rubbed the cat's neck. Over on the chair, Winter craned his neck for a better view and then tried to look uninterested. "Did you talk with him?"

"I tried, but as soon as I spoke, he disappeared. I couldn't see him, but I had the feeling he was still around. Almost like he was shy or something. I attempted to go to sleep, but the sensation that he was still in the room, just invisible, wouldn't go away. So I sat up, turned on the light, and told him that if he wanted to talk, I was there to listen."

"And what happened?"

Nick grimaced. "He appeared, but vanished again when I tried to talk with him. We played that game for about an hour, with him appearing and then doing a Houdini."

"Houdini was more of an escape artist, not a magician." When Nick glared at me I added, "Sorry."

"Anyway, I finally got the guy to speak. He was young, like I said. Just out of high school, from what I gathered. Anyway, he'd killed himself. Hanged himself in his closet over a fight with his girlfriend. There were other factors, but that was the straw that broke the camel's back. Once I got him to start talking, it all seemed to gush out. He felt so guilty for taking his own life. He didn't think he deserved to go to Heaven."

"What did you do?"

Nick sighed. "I told him that if he wanted to move on, he should. I told him that God would understand." Wearily, Nick rubbed his eyes. "I've always been an agnostic, and here I was telling a spirit that God loved him no matter what. And the funny thing was, I believed it. And the guy believed it too. He kind of smiled at me, and then the room was filled with this... this bright light. So bright that it blinded me. When the light vanished and my sight returned to normal, I was alone in the room. He was gone. I mean really gone. There wasn't a trace of him. He'd moved on." Nick turned his head to look at me. "Duncan, is there a God?"

"Hell if I know. But I'd say that if you felt it that strongly when you were talking with this ghost, then that means something. Wouldn't you say?"

A thin smile played over Nick's lips. He looked happier, but maybe even more tired. "I was hoping you'd say something like that."

I moved Jasmine aside gently and rose. "You did a good thing, Nick."

"I think I did," Nick agreed. "I couldn't get to sleep after that, but I was pretty sure I'd done something good."

"Get a nap. You need it. I'll call you later."

Nick showed me out, with Jasmine helping out. Winter stayed on the chair, looking haughty. Pissy-assed cat. At the door, he said, with a half smile, "I've got a date tonight."

Why did that make my gut feel like someone had punched it? I knew Nick had been talking about going out. But now it seemed all too real. And I was jealous. I felt horrible about it, but nonetheless I was jealous. We're all assholes sometimes. "Good," I said.

"Not sure I should go."

I forced a smile. "Go. Get some sleep, and then clean up real nice. Knock him dead."

"Thanks, Duncan. I think I will." And he hugged me. Was it my imagination, or did the hug linger a moment or two longer than a friendly hug should? Or was I projecting?

I thought about that hug as I drove home. It felt great, that human contact. I loved Robbie, but part of me still missed the touch of a fellow human being. I also thought about Nick's encounter with the spirit. I was glad he'd succeeded in encouraging a ghost to move on. After all, that's why he'd had Gina zap him. The talk about God and Heaven bothered me, though. When you deal with ghosts on a day-to-day basis, you can't help but wonder about what the afterlife actually entails. I'd become a master at dismissing these thoughts, partly because I didn't know the answers, and partly because the thoughts themselves were, in a way, painful. If there was such a place as Heaven, was I keeping Robbie from going there? Did I have that right? Would he be happy there, and was I keeping him from that happiness?

All I knew was that I wouldn't be happy without him in my life, lack of contact or not.

Duncan Andrews, you are one selfish-assed bastard.

CHAPTER 7

"I SHOULDN'T have called you."

I was glad he had. Colton Yates was in his bed, and he didn't look healthy. He was pale and his lips were redder than they should be, making the lack of color in his cheeks all that much more obvious. It was late afternoon but the room was dim, as the curtains were covering the windows. Since his boyfriend wasn't feeding off him any longer—he was currently lying in the morgue, probably giving some poor coroner the worst headache of his life—Colton's health should have improved, not gotten worse.

"I'm here to help in any way I can," I said. I sat on the side of the bed and took his hand in mine. He seemed to take some comfort in that, and attempted a smile.

"I talked to Matt's parents earlier. The police haven't released his body yet."

Carson and his cronies were still working on a way to cover up that the corpse had been dead nearly a week, no doubt. Lying and cover-ups take time to organize. "They will. Soon," I assured him.

"I still can't believe he's gone," he said. His voice was weak, and not just from grief. "I keep thinking it's all some sort of mistake and he'll walk through the door any minute now."

"I wish I could say that were true," I said. "Unfortunately...." I let the rest of the sentence go once I realized there wasn't anything really to add to the "unfortunately." What could I say? Hey, I was the one who'd pierced his heart with a pointy piece of wood. If he walked through the door right now, I'd be amazed.

Colton suddenly looked very tired. He even spoke in that slow, I'm-so-sleepy way. "That wasn't why I called you, though. I mean, I know he's dead. But, something weird happened and I didn't know anyone else to talk to. Not about this stuff."

"I'm the King of Weird. Ask anyone who knows me."

A half smile came to his face briefly, but he then turned his head toward the covered windows and his face became serious, even a little worried, as if the sun might break through the barriers and flood the room. "It's dumb, though. Forget I called you."

"Too late." I gave his hand an encouraging squeeze. "Now that I'm here, you might as well tell me. And I'm pretty sure that whatever you have to tell me, I've heard worse."

"It was a dream I had," he said, frowning. "Only it wasn't a dream. It seemed too real. But it had to be a dream. I'm not making sense."

"Tell me about it. I'll be the judge as to whether or not it makes sense. Although I'm not sure you should let me decide. I'm flummoxed every year by the income tax forms."

That brought forth a grin. It vanished quickly, but it relaxed him enough that he could continue. "Like I said, it seemed real. But... well, I'll just tell it to you and then you can call me crazy and tell me to forget it. It might all just be because of Matt, and what happened to him. Or... well, I guess you tell me."

"Sounds good."

"I went to bed early last night. I didn't figure I'd get any sleep, but I thought I might as well try. I couldn't do anything else but think about Matt. So I took a sleeping pill and lay down. I must have fallen asleep and dreamed that I was in bed. That's the only thing that makes sense. Anyway, I was just staring at the ceiling when I heard this noise outside. I figured it was just wind or something, so I ignored it, but then it came again and I realized it was my window." With his free hand he indicated the window closest to the bed. "Someone was outside, raising it. I thought it was a burglar or something. I tried to scream but I found I couldn't. My throat just wouldn't work. I even thought about my cell phone, which was next to the bed, but my arms wouldn't move. It was like I was paralyzed. I just stared at the window, which slowly opened. Then there was a dark figure scrambling inside. He got in and stood up, and I could see it was Matt's friend Braedon. One of the guys in the band." He bit his lip, obviously uncertain as to how much he wanted to tell me.

"What happened then?"

"He kind of smiled at me and then got into the bed. He was kissing me, and his hands were all over and...." He paused, looked at the window again like he expected the young man to make a reappearance. "I was never attracted to Braedon. I mean, he was okay and all that, but I never had any fantasies about him, if you know what I mean. And why would I have a dream about him, right after finding out about Matt? It didn't make any sense. And then he was ripping at my clothes, and he then he—" He stopped.

"He bit you," I said.

He nodded. "It was just a dream, though. Right? I mean, because of what Matt became. Braedon couldn't be... could he?"

"Where did he bite you?"

I didn't think he was going to reply at first. Embarrassed tears came to his eyes and he finally patted the covers just over his crotch. "Here."

"Can I see?"

Colton hesitated but then threw down the covers. He braced himself against the headboard and then shoved his boxers down. He was even skinnier than I'd thought. No waist. Tiny little hips. White, white thighs. "They don't look like bites, though. Maybe it's some mole or something that got infected."

I looked. There wasn't even a lot of pubic hair. The boy did have, however, quite an impressive penis. It was currently limp, but I could imagine what it would have been like once it had sat up and taken notice. There wasn't a trace of hair on his stomach. Colton did that thing guys do when they're at a doctor's office and the medic has to take a look at your junk. Look anywhere but at the person doing the examining.

I put a hand on his left leg, giving Colton a cue to move it a little so I could get a better look. Right at his crotch were two puncture marks. Old Braedon must have been preparing to do down on Colton's impressive dick, or actually getting some action going before sinking his nasty little fangs into the femoral vein. The wounds were partially healed, so Colton was right in that they could be taken for something other than bite marks, but I knew I wasn't seeing infected moles. Colton knew it too, but he was feeling guilty over romping in bed with Matt's bandmate. I nodded, and he yanked his boxers back up and quickly covered himself again with the sheets.

Colton's face scrunched as he lay back down. His eyes watered. "It wasn't a dream, was it?"

"No."

He closed his eyes. "Am I going to die?"

"No."

Colton shook his head. "I don't know what came over me. It was like I had no will. I didn't want Braedon in my bed, but yet I did. I mean, Matt's not even buried yet, and I was...."

"It wasn't your fault. Vampires have a way of getting into their victims' heads, a sort of hypnotism." From my experience, though, the process worked in much the way as any other kind of hypnotism. You couldn't make someone do something they didn't want to do, even under deep hypnosis. Vamp mind melds work the same way. Somewhere, in his subconscious, Colton must have wanted to have a romp in the hay with Braedon Isaacs. I wasn't going to say that, though. The poor kid felt bad enough as it was.

Colton closed his eyes tight. "Matt's not even buried, and I let his friend suck my dick and then bite me. In the groin, yet!" The eyes opened. I saw so much pain in them. "*And* suck my blood. Matt would be so...."

"Matt would have understood."

"My Matt or vampire Matt?"

I put a hand on Colton's bony shoulder. "Your Matt is the only one. He died, and then there was a vampire in his body. You've got to stop thinking of the vampire as Matt. That wasn't him anymore. Matt was a victim."

Colton was silent for quite some time. He turned his face away from me so I wouldn't see the tears. "I didn't know vampires were into fucking. I thought they just did the blood thing."

I didn't answer. One wasn't expected.

"Did Braedon do this to him? Make Matt a vampire?"

I could have explained that there were three possibilities, but Braedon was the most likely. He and Matt were friends, and Braedon had easy access to the apartment. "I think so," I said.

Colton sobbed. "I don't know what to do."

"I do. Do you trust me?"

Slowly, he nodded.

"Then we can take care of the situation tonight."

THERE was no certainty Braedon would come back that night to feed on his bandmate's boyfriend, but I had the feeling he would. After all, he hadn't waited long to chomp on him after I'd killed Matt Hamilton. Maybe our little drummer boy had the hots for Hamilton's lover, and once Matt was out of the way, he'd immediately moved in.

I wished I could move Colton off to some safe haven, but that wouldn't work. Braedon would know where he was, thanks to the psychic link between vamps and victims. A bloodsucker homing beacon, if you will. If Braedon couldn't get to Colton, he'd call him and command Colton to come.

Colton himself was feeling better as night fell, which wasn't unusual. He had been snacked on by Matt and now his friend, and was close to dying from their attacks. Another feeding or two, and he'd die from loss of blood and come back as a vampire himself. Already he had a slight aversion to sunlight. It was an even-money bet that if we paraded him in front of a mirror, his reflection would be losing coherence, as Matt's had. Soon Colton would start craving blood and finding Robert Pattinson attractive. Or maybe not on that last one, if he had taste.

Before sunset, I'd gone to Gina's for some supplies. If Gina hadn't gone off to Salem with her beau, I could have had her make a charm for Colton that would have broken or maybe even diminished the psychic link between him and Braedon, making it harder for the vamp to get at him, but you can't have everything in life. Gina had two storerooms in her place. One was stuff for her customers to buy. Love potions, good luck charms, and the like. None of those things really worked, for a good reason. Most people who came to her for, say, a love potion, really didn't know the consequences of what they were asking. A real love potion could be a dangerous thing, and if not administered correctly, could lead to the person you gave it to becoming obsessed, which could lead to stalking and downright creepiness. I knew of one case where a woman gave the guy she wanted too much of a potion, and he'd killed her and then tried to keep her corpse in his bed with him every night. I didn't even want to think about what happened with her body before neighbors started complaining about the stench and the police hauled away the dude.

The second storeroom was the real stuff—witch boxes, charms, and potions that actually worked. Among the other items there, Gina kept a supply of wooden stakes made from hawthorn trees. Gina insisted the wood from a hawthorn tree was the best to use, and who was I to argue with a witch who was around when the country was founded? I'd also gotten some fresh supplies of holy water. Where she got it, I didn't know. Maybe she'd had it shipped from Lourdes. It was good stuff, though, great for use against vampires, most demons, and a host of other creepy creatures. Just splash and sizzle.

Before returning to Colton's, I'd stopped by my place to get one more item, namely Daisy. I wanted her with me so I'd know when, and if, Braedon was in the area, so I could be prepared. Zombies don't like vampires, maybe because zombies like to feed off the living, and vampires don't come under that category. With Daisy in the room, we'd have an early warning system in place. Her instincts would kick in even before my own psychic warning system. First, though, I had to take her to the park so she could eat a few squirrel heads, as she was a hungry little bulldog.

Colton was still in bed when I returned, but was sitting up and watching television. He didn't really seem to be paying attention to the screen. I saw what was on and shook my head. I strode over to the set and flipped the channel. "*The Vampire Diaries*? No, absolutely not."

"Oh," Colton murmured. "I guess I didn't even think about it. I just always watch that program. But I guess under the circumstances, it wasn't the best choice. Inappropriate, huh?"

"It's not that. I just hate that show."

He smiled at that. The smile didn't last long, but for just the fraction of a second, I got a glimpse of the Colton Yates that had been before he got involved in this mess. A friendly young man with a good sense of humor, who liked to please people. Matt Hamilton had probably been a fairly decent boyfriend, and they'd had a good life before Matt had been drained of his blood by a vamp. My money was still on Braedon as the culprit, as he was Matt's friend. Some friend.

"What now?" he asked.

"We wait. I'd go ahead and turn off the light, though, so our friend thinks you've gone to sleep." If he showed.

He did as I suggested but stayed sitting up, his back propped against some pillows and the headboard. "Is it okay if we talk for a bit?"

"Sure."

I'd opened the curtains, so there was enough light coming in from the moon to make out his face. I was sitting in a chair near the door. Daisy was on my lap, sniffing the unfamiliar surroundings. Colton nodded toward the dog. "Is he sick or something? He doesn't look well."

"She. Her name's Daisy. And she's fine. Sort of. It's a long story."

"Her eyes look really red, especially now that the light's off. It's almost like they're glowing. It's kind of creepy."

"She's fine. Don't look if it bothers you."

Colton nodded and pulled the covers up a little. He glanced a little nervously at the window, and I thought I saw a shudder run through him. Daisy must have been a better choice than the window, because he returned his gaze to us. "So you're gay?" It was a question, not a statement.

"Yep."

"You don't look it."

"Is there a particular gay look?"

He shrugged. "I don't know. When I first went to see you, though, you didn't set off my gaydar. You're kind of intimidating. All buff and handsome. Most gay guys I know are pretty rather than handsome."

Hey, he called me buff. Did I unconsciously sit up a little straighter in the chair? "Thank you, I think."

"Do you have a boyfriend?"

"Yes, I do." Don't ask for further details, please.

"What's he like?"

"It's complicated." I didn't want to get into the whole dead boyfriend thing. Every time I tried to explain it to someone, I came off sounding like some kind of necrophiliac.

"Sorry. I didn't mean to pry."

Daisy raised her head, as if listening to sounds I couldn't hear. It must not have been alarming, for she settled back down with a snort. She rested her head on my leg, but her eyes kept moving, scanning the room. She seemed instinctively to know she was with me as a watchdog, and she was taking her duties seriously.

"How about you?" I asked, eager to change the subject. "How are you feeling?"

Colton frowned. "I'm not sure. Part of me isn't believing any of this, beginning with the fact that Matt is dead. It just doesn't seem real. And the whole Braedon thing…. If I were feeling better, I'd call you crazy and think that I was crazy as well and go out and get drunk or something. It seems like any moment I'm going to wake up from this nightmare I'm having."

Daisy's left ear twitched. In the gloom, it was hard to tell, but I think Colton sat up a little straighter. "Feeling something?" I asked.

"No," he replied. He was lying through his teeth. I could see his nervousness was being replaced with a sense of anticipation. He knew Braedon was coming.

"You can fight it," I said. "That feeling you're having, of wanting to be with him. He's projecting that feeling to you. Just ignore it."

"You're going to kill him, aren't you?" Colton's voice was losing all inflection, as if he was starting to talk in his sleep.

"Yep."

"I can feel him. Inside my head."

"That's the way it works."

Colton frowned. "What if I give you away? It's like... I don't know. Like he's forcing me to be on his side."

"You fight it," I said shortly. Colton was a nice kid, but this was no time to indulge in weenie-ness. "You just don't give in."

"He's not a bad guy. I mean, he wasn't before he died."

"He's a bad guy now. He bit your dick."

Colton laughed uneasily. "Yeah, fucking bastard. Didn't he know that vampires are supposed to go for the throat?"

"The throat is the best because they can get the jugular, but anywhere works, really. As long as they get some blood. Wrists work well too."

My mention of the biting of wrists made Colton rub his. There were no longer any visible marks, but who knew how deep the scars went? "Matt was really, really nice. I want you to know that. Before he became...." He didn't finish the sentence.

I nodded.

"He was really sweet. He made sure all the bills were paid on time and that the car was in good working order and that kind of stuff." I knew Colton was trying to ignore the messages in his brain by talking about his late boyfriend. I let him talk. If he gave into the vampire's mental messages, he might warn Braedon and ruin my plans. "When I was sick last month with the flu, Matt played nurse, bringing me ginger ale and chicken soup. It was canned chicken soup, but it's the thought that counts." His last words were barely audible, and he was now looking at the window. Unconsciously, he rubbed his crotch, right where he'd been bitten.

Daisy stiffened suddenly, and then rose and jumped to the floor. She moved a few paces toward the window, her lips curled into a snarl. Something was outside that she didn't like. It was either a vampire or Donald Trump. Whenever the Trumpster is on television, she has the same reaction. I think it's the hair. Can't blame her.

I signaled for Colton to be quiet. I'd already placed a small glass bottle of holy water on his dresser, along with a hawthorn stake. I picked these up as I moved quickly but as quietly as possible to the window, keeping to the side so that anyone looking in wasn't likely to see me.

I heard a low growl at my feet, barely audible, from Daisy. I gave her a barely audible shush in return, and she ceased. I heard her shuffle slightly as she prepared to pounce as soon as the vamp made its appearance. I have no idea why vampires affect her so. She has no trouble with ghosts and witches. But then, witches and ghosts don't smell like old gym socks or patchouli.

There was a squeak from the window as someone outside began to shove it upward. I could see an arm and then a face as Braedon pressed closer to the glass. The fingers of his right hand, which seemed preternaturally long, were slowly causing the windowpane to rise up. His eyes, black orbs in the night, were fixed on the figure in the bed. Dumbass didn't even look to see if there was a buff—official now—private detective standing off to the side, armed to the teeth with vamp-killing stuff.

That's what happens to the dead. They throw caution to the wind, thinking they're invincible. And to be fair, unless they get a pokey shaft of wood through their chests, they really are.

I held my breath as the window inched upward, watching the anticipation and hunger in Braedon's face. Out of the corner of my eye, I saw Colton, his pale forehead now beaded with sweat. He looked like he was nearly drooling. He licked his lips, and his hand came up and touched his throat. The bond between vampire and victim was strong, even overriding his grief over the death of his boyfriend. Colton swallowed hard, sitting forward now in bed. His hand went to his crotch, still covered by the sheets, and he began rubbing. This time I wasn't sure if it was unconscious or not. If the tenting of the sheet was anything to go by, I was right about Colton's dick size. His lips were parted and he seemed to be whispering something. I think it was Braedon's name over and over again, but it was so low I couldn't be sure, even though I was only about eight feet away from him.

But then his eyes strayed from the vampire's face, and shot toward me and then back to Braedon. The warning was unmistakable. The slow ascent of the window stopped as Braedon looked my way. Our eyes met. I'm pretty sure he wasn't happy to see me, especially when he also took in the stake in my left hand. The hand and face disappeared quickly, and I could hear his footsteps as he ran away.

"Damn it!"

I went to scoop up Daisy, but she was already moving. She jumped up on a chair that was close to the window. Another leap, and she was on the back of the chair and then out the window. I heard her barking as she tore away into the night. I shoved the stake into the front pocket of my jeans. The point stuck up, although I hadn't noticed which way I deposited it. At least this way I wouldn't poke a hole in my pocket and lose all my change. Daisy's barks were getting further and further away, as were the footsteps.

I only caught a fleeting glimpse of Colton as I made my way to the bedroom door. He was still sitting up, looking in turns both worried and disappointed, like he was thinking Braedon was a hell-spawn demon and needed his long hair washed, but a quick nibble wouldn't have been all that bad a thing. I didn't have time to slap him out of it. I had to move fast if I wanted to go after the vamp. I did flash him a "thanks a lot, asshole" look. And I meant it.

I ran through Colton's apartment and got to the front door. I was outside in seconds, facing the parking lot and listening for sounds of Braedon making his getaway. My breath was coming out in visible puffs of white. Then I heard Daisy, yapping like crazy. She was on the sidewalk, running as fast as her little legs would take her. Then I heard the sound of a motor revving. A motorcycle pulled out of a spot about ten or so cars away from me, and I saw the driver was wearing black and had long blond hair. Bingo!

My car was handily parked right in front of where I was standing, but I had to get Daisy first. Luckily, she had already realized she wouldn't be able to keep up with a motorcycle, and had started trotting back. There was blood on her mouth and she had a triumphant swagger to her gait. Somewhere during the chase she'd gotten close enough to take a bite out of the vamp, and she felt pretty proud about it. Unfortunately, as he was already dead, a bite from a zombie dog wouldn't affect him, but I was pleased with my little guard dog nonetheless.

I rushed forward and quickly scooped her up and the raced back to my car. I threw open the door, tossing a very cross Daisy as gently as I could—which probably wasn't as gently as I thought, but it wasn't like I could kill her again—onto the passenger seat before plopping myself behind the wheel. I dropped my stake and bottle of H-water into my lap, and fished out my keys. Ever notice how, when time is of the essence, your keys always snag on a pack of gum or something else in your pocket and you have to really yank, wasting precious seconds? Maybe that's just me. By the time I got the engine started and had backed up, I felt I'd never be able to catch up with the vamp.

Luckily, the motorcycle was loud enough that I was able to hear he'd turned left out of the apartment complex. I could even see the red taillight off in the distance. There was little traffic, which was a good thing, as I stomped on the gas halfway through my turn and nearly fishtailed up onto the sidewalk. I regained control and took off in pursuit.

My eyes never left the red taillight ahead of me, but I was aware that there was a disgruntled bulldog sitting next to me. "Sorry, Daisy," I told her. "You might want to find something to hold on to. This could get nasty."

Moments later, I had to take a sharp right turn, somehow managing to miss a Ford coming toward us. Daisy let out a yelp and tumbled to the floorboard. Out of the corner of my eye, I could see a flurry of legs and a plump body rolling, but she seemed unhurt by the fall. She did, however, decide it was safer staying off the seat.

Ahead of us, the motorcycle was speeding up. He was heading closer to the downtown area, and now there were more cars on the road. Horns blasted in annoyance as first a motorcycle and then my Mustang that had seen better days wove in and out of traffic. I didn't bother to look at the speedometer, but I was pretty sure we weren't doing the posted thirty-mile-an-hour speed limit. In my head, I was already explaining things to a bewildered cop. *Yes, that's right, officer. I was chasing a vampire on a motorcycle. A real bat cycle, if you will.* It would almost be worth it to be stopped just so I could have that conversation.

Ahead, Braedon took a right onto Tenth Street. I had closed up the gap between us enough that I saw him nearly collide with an SUV in the intersection. In order to miss the other vehicle, he had to turn sharper than he'd intended, and his back wheel slid dangerously close to a parked car. The maneuver caused his motor to stall, and it took him several seconds to get the thing going again. Now I was almost on his ass. He even glanced back to see how close I was before speeding off down Tenth, nearly clipping a station wagon coming out of a Shell station. The wagon's driver slammed on the brakes, and added the sound of his horn to the cacophony that accompanied the chase.

"Sorry, Dais," I said as I wrestled with the wheel and spun us onto Tenth. "I've got to catch this bastard. Not only is he a vampire, but he's riding a motorcycle without a helmet, and that's just damned unsafe." Daisy let out an angry bark, but I'm sure it was because she was being slammed against the passenger door and not because of my bad joke.

More horns blared as I saw the motorcycle shoot around a car and veer into the lane of oncoming traffic. One car, in order to avoid a wreck, had to brake hard. The car behind him, though, had been going too fast to stop in time, and there was a crunch of metal as the first car got rear-ended. I could hear the driver of the second car screaming obscenities out his window as I raced by them.

Braedon was now nearly to Meridian Street, and I figured I had him. Meridian was busy enough, even at this time of night, that he'd almost certainly have to slow down to get across, or end up as vampire splat on the pavement. It wouldn't kill him, but even a vampire would have to take time to heal from something like that. Sure enough, I saw his brake light come on as he approached the intersection.

I had him. But then I saw an old man with a long beard step off the curb only several hundred yards ahead of me. To my left was a delivery van coming my way. How the old man missed the motorcycle weaving through traffic doing ninety on a busy street, I don't know, but he seemed oblivious to any danger. He certainly didn't see my Mustang barreling toward him.

I stomped on the brakes and twisted the wheel to the right so that I would miss both the old man and the delivery van. Unfortunately, this meant I had to go up over the curb and right into a lamppost. Every bone in my body felt as if it had been jerked right out of my skin and remained somewhere about ten feet behind where the car finally stopped. My head flew forward but the airbag deployed, so I didn't hit the steering wheel. One second there was the steering wheel in front of me, and the next my vision was filled with white airbag. I can't honestly say if I hit the airbag or it hit me. And while I can't say it was like leaping face first into a mound of soft, fluffy pillows, I can't say it hurt either. I'm sure it was a damn sight better than hitting the steering wheel.

As I sat there taking mental inventory—was I dead, was anything broken, and could someone shut off that fucking car horn, oh, it's mine, never mind—I heard an angry bark next to me and then felt a dry tongue licking my wrist.

"Sorry about that, Daisy," I said. The words sounded like my mouth was full of marbles.

She barked. I had the feeling that she was telling me she would have preferred that I'd have chosen to make road chum out of the old man, rather than introducing the front of the Mustang to a now toppled lamppost.

This was going to be a fun insurance claim.

CHAPTER 8

I NEARLY fell into the apartment, like a dead body in a murder mystery. Somehow I managed to stay erect, and I even succeeded in tossing my keys into the little bowl on the stand by the door, something I often can't do even when my body hasn't been pummeled into Jell-O. Daisy was at my feet and was in more of a hurry to get inside to familiar surroundings, so she darted between my legs with a few excited barks. Other than being tossed around a bit, she hadn't sustained any damage from the crash—a good thing, as zombies don't do the healing thing very well—but it would be ages before I'd convince her not every car trip resulted in *that* sudden of a stop.

Standing behind me was Nick, who had given me a ride home from the hospital, where I'd been checked out and given a clean bill of health. The doctor who'd examined me had raised his eyebrows when I responded to his query as to why I was there with the answer that I'd driven my car eighty-five miles an hour into a lamppost, but he hadn't signed me up for an extended stay in the psych ward, so I was grateful. I walked away with only a headache, a few bruises, and one cut nicely bandaged up. My left knee had suffered the worst.

Nick touched my elbow to let me know he was there for support if I decided to suddenly collapse. "You doing okay?" he asked.

"Peachy." I walked gingerly over to the couch on legs that didn't seem to want to move correctly. I felt like I was a Claymation figure in an old *Gumby* short. I winced as I sat down. Daisy went right to the kitchen and her water bowl. I never knew why a zombie bulldog would still have a need for water, but I could hear her lapping up the stuff like there was no tomorrow. Which, come to think of it, would be fine with me. I felt like hell. Hell on a bad day.

Robbie appeared, standing over me with a concerned expression. "What the hell have you been doing?"

I rubbed my eyes. My eyelids felt like they'd been gone over with coarse sandpaper. "Do you want the full story or the abridged version?"

"Abridged for now."

"I was out wrecking the car."

He blinked. "Maybe I'd better get the full version."

"I was out wrecking the car into a lamppost."

Robbie nodded. "Well, that cleared that up."

As Nick sat down in an armchair adjacent to me, I reported the events of the night to Robbie. Technically, as it was now morning, the night before. I finished with, "I had to get Lieutenant Carson involved in order not to be charged with reckless endangerment and a host of other citations. He wasn't happy to be roused in the middle of the night. But then, I'm not sure he's ever happy. Then I got checked out at the hospital, which luckily was just down the road from where I'd had my little fender bender—"

"The car was totaled," Nick interjected.

"Yes, thank you. The fact that the radiator ended up in the front seat may have been a clue that repairs might have been extensive, to say the least."

I would have said Robbie's face paled, but with a ghost you can never tell. "You killed the car?" he said weakly.

"It died a noble death."

"And the vamp got away?"

I made a face, my one that said, *Really, you're going there?* "He kept going. Rude-ass bastard. Least he could have done was to turn around and checked to see if Daisy was all right."

"Daisy was in the car with you?" Concern over me was replaced with worry for the dog. Robbie looked around and spotted

Daisy walking out of the kitchen, licking her lips. Drops of water and saliva splattered onto the floor.

"Relax. She's fine. Maybe a little hungry. Nick watched after her while I was being checked out."

"Fine with me," Nick muttered. "I hated being in the hospital." When Robbie glanced questioningly at him, he added, "There were too many spirits in there! I must have seen at least four ghosts in just the few minutes it took me to find out where Duncan was!"

"Well, yeah," Robbie said. "People die in hospitals. There are bound to be a few lingering around, trying to decide what to do."

"Can we focus here, people?" I asked, raising my voice just a tad. "I was just in an auto accident. I'm tired and bitchy and I feel like a steamroller plowed over everything except my toes, the only part of my body that doesn't hurt. Someone should at least offer to get me a soda."

Nick looked uncertainly up at Robbie, who said, "Hey, you're corporeal. You get it." Nick nodded quickly and got up went to the kitchen. When he'd gone, Robbie sat down on the arm of the couch and ran his fingers through my hair, which was a nice gesture as, while I couldn't really feel his fingers, it did have the effect of cooling my forehead. "So where are we?"

"We've still got three vampires, at least, in town. I don't think our friend Braedon will try for Colton again now that he knows we're onto him, but I'd like to convince him to leave town and visit relatives for a while just in case. Lieutenant Carson so far hasn't been able to come up with current addresses for Braedon or Kissy Peters—"

"Kissy?" Robbie asked.

"Real name Jennifer."

"Thank God. I was going to have harsh words with her parents."

"Anyway, I do have an address for Jennifer Peter's parents, as well as the parents of Braedon Isaacs. Strangely, there's no record of a Dominic Hunt, not that fits the description anyway. I'm guessing he's the daddy vamp, the one that converted the others. He's probably very, very old, which means he's picked up a trick or two in his time and he'll be a bitch to kill."

Robbie smiled encouragingly. "You'll do it. You can do anything."

"Really? Because I seem to be having trouble keeping my eyes open."

"Sleep now. Kill vampires later." He tugged at my arm. I almost felt it. "Come on, big guy. Bed for you."

I wanted to act as if I wasn't fazed by the events of the evening and be all "Oh, I'm fine," but the truth was I felt like I could fall asleep any second, and my bed would feel better than the couch. I rose slowly and stiffly as Nick returned with a glass filled with ice and soda. "Change of plans," I told him. "Drink that yourself. I'm going to sleep."

"Oh." He looked at the glass as if wondering how it got to be in his hands.

"There is something you can do for me while I snooze, though."

"Name it," Nick said.

"Daisy is probably starving. Could you take her to the park so she can get a bite?"

Nick gulped. He knew Daisy's meal of choice. He also knew that when she finished eating, her maw was covered with blood and brain matter, and she had to be quickly cleaned up before people in the park—those without zombie dogs—could see her.

"I really must," Nick said, more to himself than to us, "not be so quick to agree to do things where you guys are concerned."

THE fire alarm was going off.

Or maybe it was just my cell phone. I stirred and rolled onto my side, but made no effort to reach over to the nightstand and answer the call. I didn't feel like moving my arms, and they agreed with me. The phone kept up with its annoying chirp, however, and seemed to sound more insistent with each ring. Finally, with a groan, I reached over and fumbled around until my fingers located the damn thing.

"Hello?" I said. "And before you answer, I must warn you that if you are a telemarketer, I may have to kill you."

"My, we're sounding cheery this evening!"

I frowned. My fogged brain began to function, although it was still very confused. Evening? I looked at the window. The sun had said good-bye to the day and night had fallen. How long had I slept?

"Gina," I said, trying not to sound like one of the orcs in *Lord of the Rings*. "Sorry. I was just taking a little nap."

"You don't take naps."

I also don't crash my cars into lampposts, but things change. "Rough day. But how are you?"

"Missing you, of course, but it feels good to be having a vacation. The town may have changed over the years, but it's still Salem. It's still home. And it feels strangely comforting."

"That's good. Now for the big question. Have you told Mark?"

"I have."

I knew that the result hadn't been catastrophic, or her tone wouldn't have been so upbeat, but she obviously wanted to drag out the news. I played along. "And?"

"He took it well. Of course there was a lot of confusion at first, and I had to convince him that I wasn't some Wiccan or a weird sort of pagan that danced nude around a campfire at midnight waving palm fronds."

"You *do* dance around campfires nude. I've seen you."

"Yes, but only for fun. And then I had to assure him that it wasn't some kind of *Bewitched* thing where all I had to do was twitch my nose and poof, suddenly Dick York is a cat."

"I must have missed that episode."

I propped myself up on one elbow. My head was clearing and the world was falling back into place. Robbie was beside me in bed, twisted around so that he could watch me while I chatted on the phone. He was lying on top of the covers, wearing his usual basketball shorts.

"So he took it well?" I wasn't exactly surprised, as I knew Mark worshiped the ground Gina walked on, and that if she told him she was the Masked Avenger, he would have gone along with it, but I was still impressed. Good guy, Mark the Dentist. "How exactly did you explain it to him?"

"We were just strolling down the street and we passed some window with a poster of a wart-nosed hag on a broomstick in the window. I told him it was such an incorrect depiction and went on from there. Naturally he thought I was kidding at first."

"Naturally."

"Finally, he believed me."

"How did you convince him? I mean, if I was a normal Joe Blow and someone told me they were a witch, I'd assume they were cuckoo."

"And I'm sure he thought that at first and was merely humoring me. But as we walked along, we came along a little bird that had broken its wing. I healed it. Well, gave it enough mojo that it was mostly healed, anyway, and the thing managed to fly away. That helped lend credence to my story. Mark's still digesting the information, but so far the reaction has been favorable. He's not running to the airport to get the next flight back, anyway. Mind you, when we went to a bar for some cocktails, I'd never seen anyone down a martini quite so fast. How are things on your end?"

I told her, at least the hot points. She commiserated with me over the death of my car and we chatted for another minute or so. Finally, she said, "Well, I'd better go. Mark's probably ready for our night out on the town by now. Give my love to Robbie and kill those vamps for me."

I promised her I would, and ended the call. I put the phone back on the nightstand and settled back on my pillow, staring up at the ceiling.

"Penny for your thoughts," Robbie said.

"You'd be overcharged."

He snuggled up closer to me. I could feel the air around me getting colder as he drew in energy. He looked so solid that it was impossible to believe that, if I tried to wrap my arms around him, all I'd feel was a cold breeze. He leaned in close and pursed his lips. I did the same, our lips touching, and for a moment, I could feel his lips against mine. I closed my eyes, remembering the long, loving kisses we'd enjoyed when we were both young and alive. God, I missed those days. I wanted to draw him into me and make sweet love to him, but that was denied us. Robbie ended the kiss and moved his head back, keeping his eyes on mine.

"Something's troubling you. What is it? Fess up."

"Nothing really."

"The more you deny that something's bothering you, the more I know that something is." He reached over and took my hand in his. Again, for just a second there was actual contact, but then it just felt like a cobweb was brushing against my hand. "Is it the car? The fact that the vamp got away?"

"Those are both good, but I think what Nick's going through is the main thing that's bugging me."

"The seeing ghosts thing? He seems to be getting used to it."

I shook my head. "It's the whole getting ghosts to move on thing. It all goes back to that Ricky Vallis guy." We had met television star Ricky Vallis on a previous case. We hadn't gotten along, partially because Vallis had been convinced Robbie should move on, and partially because he was an asshole.

Robbie shifted onto his back so we were both staring up at the ceiling. "If ghosts want to move on and need a little encouragement, I don't see anything wrong with it. Nick's just helping them out." He squeezed my hand, and again I felt the contact for a moment. "Are you worried that he's going to try to get me to move on?"

"He wouldn't dare," I said with a slight smile. "Still, we don't really know what happens when a ghost moves on. Maybe there's nothing and we're sending them to oblivion."

"You don't really believe that."

I sighed. "No, I don't. I've seen too much to not think that there's something beyond this life. I just don't know what it is."

"Maybe we're not supposed to." Robbie released my hand, and folded his arms across his chest. He did it unconsciously, merely relaxing, but I wondered if he realized he resembled a corpse in its coffin.

"I just wish I knew what was the right thing to do. Maybe by asking you to stay here, I'm keeping you from your destiny or something. I just don't know."

"You don't hear me complaining, do you?"

"You wouldn't." I sighed again, deeper this time. "I just don't know what to do. I love you, and I always will, but how much longer can we go on like this?"

"I love you too," he replied. "And you know, no matter what happens, a part of me will always be here with you. If you think it's time for me to move on—"

"I… I just…. It's just not a decision I'm prepared to make. Not yet."

Robbie turned onto his side and kissed me again. This time I just felt the brush of cold against my lips, but it was the thought that counted. "You just let me know when you're ready. It's your call."

"Thanks. I needed that extra responsibility."

His face was full of love. "I'll always be here for you. That's really all that matters, isn't it?"

I BORROWED Gina's car to use until I could get a replacement for the Mustang. It was an old, battered Chevy Nova that always sounded like it didn't want to start, and would only get you from point A to point B in spite of itself. Apparently her healing abilities didn't extend to car engines, as this one was on its last leg. I spent a productive day chatting amiably with my insurance company—if calling them "you fuckers" counts as an amiable conversation— going over events with Lieutenant Carson—"I'm running out of ways to bail you out of shit like this!"—and having a burger at a fast food restaurant. Lunch was the most productive part. I then called Colton Yates and tried to get him to spend time out of town, with a relative or some friend. He appreciated the advice, but I could tell he wasn't going to take it. He wanted to stay in town for Matt Hamilton's funeral, which had finally been arranged.

My calls all done, I stopped at a truck stop to take a whizz. At the line of urinals, I was standing next to a bearded trucker type who smelled vaguely of sweat and chicken soup, when my cell phone chirped. My ringtone was the theme from *The Twilight Zone*, and out of the corner of my eye, I saw the trucker dude giving me an odd look. I smiled—to myself, not to the trucker, so as not to give an impression I might regret—and tried to urge the stream of piss to go faster. I somehow managed to get myself zipped back up and my hands washed before the call went to my voice mailbox. I was standing at the sink, aware that the trucker guy was still at his urinal, listening to every word.

"Hello," I said, with that "didn't you know I was pissing" tone that one uses in such situations.

It was Lieutenant Carson. He didn't sound happy. I wondered if he ever did. "We've got something."

There seemed like there should be more to his announcement, but he was obviously waiting for me to ask, so I did. "What do you got?"

"A possible address for Braedon Isaacs. He hasn't been there for over a month, but he had been living with a guy named Laramie Fitzgerald. I was just going to go and ask him a few questions, and thought you might like to tag along."

"Why, Lieutenant, you've never invited me to an interrogation before. I'm flattered." The trucker dude had finished but was taking his time zipping up, not wanting to miss my conversation. "I'm not in town right now, but I can be there fairly quickly."

"I figured it might be handy to have you there, just in case. You might pick up on any weird things."

"Weird things?" Oh, now the trucker was really interested.

94

"You know. Just in case this Fitzgerald guy turns out to be a vampire or a werewolf or some fucking demon."

"Why should he be any of those?"

"I don't know!" Carson exploded. "Whenever you show up, people get wooden stakes through their hearts or get eaten by zombies or become weird-ass monsters at the drop of a hat! And who has to cover things up so the public doesn't panic? Me! So I thought I'd have you along to talk to this guy just in case he goes for my throat, or worse. I think you owe me that much, Andrews!"

I nodded, which was a strange thing to do when you're talking on the phone. "Fucking demons. I've dealt with them before."

"What?"

"Demons who fuck. Quite a lot. Very unpleasant creatures, but it's easy to catch them with their pants down, so to speak."

I at least got Carson calmed down a little. Interested, he asked, "Really? There are demons who do that? Fuck all the time?"

"Yeah. I call them Kardashians."

Carson groaned. "Call me when you're back in town." He hung up.

I pocketed my cell phone and looked at the trucker dude. "Sorry about that. Important call."

He nodded slowly. I walked out of the restroom and he followed me, not having washed his hands. Some people were just so unsanitary.

A SHORT while later, I was standing with Lieutenant David Carson in the hallway of an apartment complex near IUPUI, which stands for Indiana University-Purdue University Indianapolis, but that's too long to say, so everyone just uses the letters or sounds them out. Ooeepooie. IUPUI sounds better. We found apartment 3E, and Carson knocked on the door. While we waited to see if anyone answered, Carson said, "If anyone asks, you're officially helping the police with their inquiries into the death of Matt Hamilton."

"Really? Official? Do I get money for that?"

"No."

"Do I have to sign something to make it official?" I loved teasing the lieutenant, and I was sure he adored being teased. It gave him an excuse to groan, which he so obviously loved.

"Nope. I just say it, and it's official."

We heard someone shuffling inside, coming to the door. "It must be interesting to wield that much power," I said.

"Frightening," Carson said as the door opened.

We were greeted by a young man who could have been anywhere between sixteen and twenty-five. He wasn't tall, but I wouldn't say he was short. He wasn't fat, but neither was he fit. It was like the guy couldn't commit to anything physically. He had a cherubic face and tightly curled reddish-blond hair. "Yes?"

Carson was standing in front of me. He had pulled out his wallet and was showing his badge. I pulled mine out as well, but it showed my Kroger Plus card. Not as impressive, but the kid wasn't paying attention to me anyway. His eyes were fixed on Carson's badge, and I had the distinct feeling he hoped he hadn't left his stash out where it could be seen.

Carson was trying to look friendly and reassuring, and not being very successful at either. "I'm Lieutenant Carson and this is Duncan Andrews. We're looking for Laramie Fitzgerald."

The kid gulped. "Yeah? What about?"

"Just want to ask you a few questions. We're looking into the death of Matt Hamilton."

"But I thought Matt was killed in some drug deal gone wrong. That's what it said on the news."

I hadn't realized that was the story that had been released. I really had to stop getting all my news from Jon Stewart and *The Daily Show*, and pick up a newspaper once in a while. Hopefully I didn't have my "you're kidding" face on, or Carson would be really pissed, and with good reason.

"We want to ask you some questions about your former roommate, Braedon Isaacs. May we come in?"

The apartment was furnished in hand-me-downs and beer cans. There was also a bong in the corner on the floor by a ratty-looking chair, but if Carson noticed it, he let it go. Carson didn't take off his coat, so I left my jacket on as we sat on the couch. I could feel the springs poking into my buttocks. Laramie Fitzgerald sat in the chair and surreptitiously shoved the bong out of sight. He looked nervous. Couldn't say I blamed him. Carson made me nervous and we were on the same side. Sort of.

"How can I help?" Laramie asked.

"We're trying to track down the members of the band that Matt Hamilton was in. Ask them what happened that night. Only they all seem to have disappeared." Carson cocked his head sideways on the last word he spoke, giving the impression that he thought Laramie was somehow involved.

The boy licked his lips. "I haven't seen Braedon in weeks."

Carson nodded. "Know where he might be?"

"No," Laramie answered. He was fidgeting with his hands, rubbing kinks out of knuckles that probably didn't have kinks in them.

"How about the other members of the band he was in?" Carson pulled a little notebook out of his pocket as if he needed to check the names, although I would bet the action was just for show. "Jennifer Peters or Dominic Hunt. Know where we might find them?"

Laramie shook his head. "No idea."

Carson stared at the kid for a moment, his intent clear. *You're not giving me the answers that I want and I don't like it, kid.* "Is Braedon's mail being forwarded anywhere?"

"No," the kid said, shaking his head. The room wasn't that warm, but a bead of sweat was showing on his forehead. Carson picked up on that and just stared at Laramie, knowing the boy would get even more nervous and finally speak up. It worked. "That is, I may know where Kissy was staying. I mean Jennifer." He looked down, embarrassed. "She preferred to go by Kissy."

Carson was deadpan. "And the address."

Laramie gave it to us. Carson jotted it down in his notebook. "But I'm not sure it's where she's living," the kid went on. "I'm pretty sure, because she had a party there. I went, but didn't stay long. There was a kind of creepy vibe going on, so I left. I haven't seen her since."

"And when was this party?"

"Last Friday." Just a day before I had my tussle with Matt Hamilton in the alley. "The band was playing, The Scarlet Tide. I really didn't know too many people there, and they were mostly Goth types. Not my kind of scene."

Carson closed his notebook and rose slowly. I followed suit. He looked at me to see if I had anything to add. I didn't. Carson said to the kid, "If you have anything to add, get in touch with me." He handed Laramie his card.

Back out in the hallway, Carson glared at me. "You were a lot of help back there."

"I was just marveling at your people skills," I said. "Plus, I was poised, ready to attack if he became a bloodsucking fiend and leaped at you."

Carson sighed and then gave me something resembling a smile. "I'm not really trained to deal with vampires and the supernatural. I like things I can shoot and they fall dead. What now? Should we go check out this house?"

"It's daytime. She won't answer if she is there."

He made a sour face. "I have to do something. I can't just sit around twiddling my thumbs."

"Can't hurt to check the place out. If she is staying there, I'd like to get the layout of the place. That, and break in and see if I can stake her while she's sleeping. It's much easier that way. When they're awake, they wiggle and squirm and fight back. Very strenuous."

Carson raised his eyebrows. "Breaking and entering? You know I can't condone that. I'd need a warrant, and I certainly can't go to the judge and say I'm on the track of vampires."

"Turn your back, then. Smoke a cigarette or something. You'd just get in the way, anyhow."

Carson rolled his eyes, and turned to lead the way back to his car. "I should have thrown you in a padded cell when I first met you," he grumbled.

"But then you'd have missed my witty banter," I replied. He didn't reply.

THE house in question was on the west side of town, not far from Eagle Creek Park, where I'd once taken Daisy to their dog park, which hadn't gone well when she mistook a small Yorkie for a squirrel. The Yorkie survived the encounter, but the tongue-lashing I got from the owner ended up with me and my dog being banned from the dog park in perpetuity.

It wasn't an easy house to find. Carson had to backtrack once to get to the right road, and even then we were sure we were going the wrong way, as the residential section ended and we were in a heavily wooded area. Finally a house loomed ahead of us, a two-story affair that had once been painted white. Most of the paint had peeled or faded, and now the place looked old and gray. There was a bench swing on the porch that was moving gently with the breeze. When we went up the steps and onto the porch, the boards creaked in protest. One step had a hole in it that we had to avoid, and even then, I was afraid the remaining steps wouldn't hold the weight of either me or Carson. They did.

Carson knocked on the front door, and as expected, no one answered. We waited a good two minutes before he looked at me and asked, "Now what?"

There was a rusted mailbox affixed to the wall by the door. I opened the lid. Nothing there. "Does this look like a house that someone lives in?"

"Looks abandoned to me."

We walked around. The grass didn't look like it had been mowed all summer, and there were several rosebushes along the side of the house, mostly dead. "*Better Homes and Gardens* probably isn't ready to do a spread on this place," I said.

The backyard was even more overgrown. There was an old tractor tire in the middle of the yard, and an old Chevy with no hood and no tires. Surrounding the yard was a wire fence that was the only thing on the property that didn't look like it was falling apart. Beyond the fence was a big drop off, almost a cliff. I wandered over and looked down. Below was another house, this one a small cottage surrounded by a picket fence. It didn't look like it was lived in either.

"Nice neighborhood," I said. "The block parties must be a scream."

Carson had found something in the grass. He picked it up, realized it was part of a muffler, and tossed it aside. "If I were to pick a house that was haunted, though, this would be it. I wouldn't want to spend the night here."

"There's electricity, though. Still hooked up."

"How do you know that?"

"We passed the meter. It was running. Plus, Fitzgerald said the band played at the party he went to. You need electricity for guitars and such."

Again, he almost smiled. "My, aren't you just a regular Sherlock Holmes."

I looked back at the house. The windows were grimy and most of them had no curtains, but there was no evidence of furniture inside. I sauntered up to one, which turned out to be a kitchen window, cupped my hands, and peered inside. I couldn't see much. A wooden table with a plate on it. The plate was chipped. One cupboard door was open, revealing bare shelves. If anyone was residing in the house, they weren't doing much eating. Drinking, maybe.

"See anything interesting?"

Carson had come up behind me so quietly, I almost jumped out of my skin. "No convenient coffins lying around, no," I said, recovering.

He nodded, an amused smile playing over his lips at seeing me start. "I can go back to the car, check to see who owns the house and who's paying the electric bill. Might take some time. Fifteen, twenty minutes."

"Could it take thirty?"

"It could."

"And I won't break in and search the place while you're doing that, because that would be wrong."

Carson nodded again and walked away. As soon as he was out of sight, I checked the back door. Locked, but the wood looked old and flimsy. A good few kicks would get me in, but I didn't want to announce I'd been there, if at all possible. I went back to the kitchen window and put my hands against the glass and pushed up. It creaked and protested, but opened.

I was glad Carson wasn't there to see, because there's really no way to haul yourself into a house via the window and still look dignified. I basically just went in head first, wiggled and squirmed a bit, and slid down the inside wall as best I could. It worked, that's about the best you could say about it.

After dusting myself off, I went through each room fairly quickly, just to get the layout of the place. The housekeeper should've been fired. There wasn't much there, and what was there was covered in grime. There was a refrigerator in the kitchen that was still hooked up, which had something that may have once been a head of lettuce in it and a jar of jalapeno peppers. Hell of a salad. There were a few pots and pans stored away, a thin film of dust covering them. In one of the front rooms was a couch that looked like it had been rescued from a dumpster and a chair with three legs.

There were five bedrooms, three of which were totally empty. One contained a few boxes, mostly empty, a broken model of the Millennium Falcon, and a paperback edition of an old Perry Mason mystery. The price had been twenty-five cents.

The other bedroom, one upstairs and facing the back, was more interesting. It contained a dresser, empty, an old lamp with a shade that even my grandmother would have said was too gaudy, and a bed. The bed looked like someone had occupied it not too long ago. The sheets, while not clean, were at least in better shape than the rest of the house. There was a brass headboard that had leather restraints attached to it, and the pillowcase had a few flecks of blood on it.

Someone had been tied up here and used as an occasional snack.

The closet gave me a clue as to who it had been. There was a jacket on a wire hanger, the only article of clothing there. The jacket was that of a small man's. I searched the pockets and found a grocery list, a receipt from Taco Bell, and a crumpled photograph. The photograph showed Braedon Isaacs and Laramie Fitzgerald hugging each other in a way that told me they had been more than just friends. In the photo, Braedon was wearing the jacket I was searching.

Well, now I knew why Braedon had vanished from Laramie's apartment. He'd been kidnapped by one of the vamps, and used as food until he'd died and become a bloodsucker himself.

I still had the attic and the basement to search, but it would be dark soon and I didn't have my fun vamp-killing stuff with me. I went downstairs and unlocked the front door, and went out that way. I could have wiggled back through the kitchen window, but I didn't want to get stuck in it like Winnie the Pooh after the honey. Plus I just didn't want to.

Carson was leaning against the car, seemingly bored. He raised his eyebrows when I approached. "Find anything?"

"Enough."

"The house belongs to one Lenore Peters, who is Jennifer's aunt. She moved out three months ago and is planning on selling the place, but she hasn't got around to listing it yet. She's kept the power on because her niece is staying at the house until she finds a place of her own. Lenore's been paying the electric, gas, and water bills."

"You talked with her?"

Carson rolled his eyes. "No, I held a séance and spoke with her late husband who filled me in on all the details. Of course I talked with her. Did you think I was out here jerking off while you had your little fun in there? Got the info and called her. The police may not be experts on the supernatural, but we have some uses."

"What now?"

He shrugged. "Well, I know that I can't go up there and knock on the door and expect her to answer, if what you're telling me is true. And I can get a search warrant, but I don't know what good that will do either. Vampires are outside my field of expertise."

"So if I came back here in an hour and took care of things, that would be okay with you?"

"Unofficially," he said slowly, not looking at me, "I'd appreciate it."

"WISH I could go with you."

Robbie was following me as I packed my duffel bag with my crossbow, arrows, stakes, and other vamp-killing paraphernalia. The bag was on the bed, and I was filling it from my stash in a chest in the closet. "Not one of your usual haunts, I'm afraid. Besides, there's really nothing you could do to help."

"Moral support?" The trips back and forth were taking their toll on his energy, so he sat on the bed next to the bag. "And there's always the helpful hint. You know, shouting out, 'Hey, there's a vampire behind you,' and keeping you from getting ambushed."

"Like a vampire could sneak up behind me." I pulled an old flintlock pistol out of the chest and eyed it questioningly. "What the hell's that doing in there?" Not expecting an answer, I tossed it back into the chest and instead grabbed another, smaller crossbow.

"They've done it before," Robbie said.

"Once, when I was distracted." I returned to the bed, and had to rearrange things in the duffel to make room for the second crossbow. "Always good to have a backup," I said, "just in case the first one decides to be all French and just give up."

"I know you're just joking, but historically the French have won more battles than...." He broke off when he saw my glare. "I watch the History Channel a lot."

"I was kidding. I like the French."

"How many do you know?"

I paused. "Does Jean-Luc Picard count?"

Robbie made a sour face. "Try one that isn't fictional and played by a British actor. Are we going to talk about what's really bothering you?"

I frowned as I tried to zip up the bag. It wasn't a huge carryall and the crossbows bulged out, making closing the bag tricky, but with some extra shoving, I managed it. "Why do you think something is bothering me?"

"You haven't looked at me once during this conversation."

I looked up, realizing he was right. I shoved the bag to one side and sat down next to him. "I'm not sure there's anything to talk about, and if there were, I'm sure this isn't the best time. I'm about to go out vamp hunting."

"And what if you get killed? It could happen, you know. Despite what you think, you're not invincible."

"Then we'll both be ghosts and we can talk then."

"New Year's Eve," Robbie said.

I blinked. "That came out of nowhere. What about New Year's Eve?"

"That's when I'm going to pass over to the other side."

That cold, hard feeling in my chest returned, making my heart feel like a rock. I had to force myself not to look away from him. "What are you talking about? What brought this on?"

He smiled gently. "Duncan, I've been dead for over eleven years now."

"You should be getting used to it by now, then."

He ignored the quip. Can't say I blamed him. "We both know that we've put off this decision for too long now. And that you'll never think it's the right time. And I thought that if we set a date, we could both get used to the idea. At first, I thought Christmas, but that would suck. You don't want Christmas to be a downer. But New Year's would be good. Fresh start. We could both move on."

I blinked again, but this time to keep back the tears that were threatening to spill. "I don't see why we have to plan something like that. We'll know when the time is right."

Robbie reached over and placed his hand on mine. "You can barely feel my fingers on yours. All you really feel is a cold sensation over your hand."

"So?" I looked away, fixing my gaze on my dresser. There was no way I could look at his face and say the next sentence. "I love you. I don't see why we have to change anything."

"That's just it," he said softly. "I love you too. And I always will. That will never change. But we've let our love get in the way of moving on with our lives." He paused, and I could sense the smile even though I didn't see it. "Well, your life. Mine ended years ago. Which is sort of the point."

I didn't want to continue with the conversation, but I didn't say so, because Robbie would merely reply with "you never do" or something similar. True, but it didn't change my feelings. So I stood up and went over to my dresser and opened the top drawer. All for show, because it was my sock and underwear drawer. I was just pretending to be busy. What was I going to do, pack an extra pair of undies in case a vamp literally scared the shit out of me, or put on my lucky vamp-killing socks?

When I didn't reply, Robbie asked, "Have you ever thought about what Heaven is like?"

"No." The answer came automatically, and it was a lie. Of course I had. Who hadn't? Having a dead boyfriend that was still hanging around, maybe I'd thought about it more than most.

His voice was wistful. "I read somewhere that Heaven was a place where, as soon as you entered, all the dogs that ever loved you in your lifetime came up to greet you." During his pause, I closed the top drawer and opened the next one down. T-shirts. I looked at them as if surprised to find them there. Robbie continued. "Daisy's dead, but she's still here. Just like me. I wonder if she'll be up there to greet me, or if I'll have to wait until the two of you show up."

I couldn't take any more. "Can we talk about something else? The Cubs, or who would win in a fight, Gandalf or Batman?"

"No, we can't. And it would so be Batman."

I closed the T-shirt drawer. "I've got to go and kill some vampires. If you want to sit around here and talk morbid, you can do it on your own."

"We don't have to talk about it, but I just want you to know it's going to happen. New Year's Eve. Maybe even on the stroke of twelve! New adventures for the both of us."

I turned to face him. "You'd leave me alone?"

He was smiling at me with such a sad smile, it was impossible to be annoyed with him. "You wouldn't be alone. You've got Nick."

"Nick's just a friend."

"Right now he is. But that's only because I'm holding you back. I know you like him. Without me here, that might develop into something else."

"He's dating someone else. Or at least met someone else."

"He won't be dating them for long. He really likes you. I can see that. You can too. You just choose to ignore it." Robbie pulled his legs up and hugged his knees. He got an almost dreamy expression on his face. "We'll have a big party for my going away. That's the way to do it. And the way to look at it. My going-away party. Come on, Dunc. Even you have to admit that it's been obvious our relationship has been going on borrowed time for quite some time now."

"I can't argue with you right now," I said as I went over and grabbed my duffel bag. My legs felt weird, as if it was someone else walking and I was just going along for the ride. He was making sense and being very rational, but the heart wasn't a rational thing. However, I had things to do, and if he was really serious—and he seemed to be—about this New Year's thing, I had two months to talk him out of it.

"I've got to go."

He rose and came over to me. He put his arms around me. Maybe it was because our emotions were so intense, but I could feel his strength as he hugged me. I could feel the arms encircling me. When he kissed me, I could feel his lips. The sensation didn't last, for as soon as our lips parted, he was once again as insubstantial as usual. "I'll always love you, Duncan."

I held him, or at least what I could feel of him. I closed my eyes.

Killing vampires, easy. A relationship with a ghost was a bitch.

CHAPTER 9

I WAS trying to make a quick getaway, but fate had a way of plonking down in front of you and saying, "Not so fast, asshole." When I opened the front door to leave, I found an envelope neatly taped just below the peephole.

"What's that?" Robbie asked.

I turned it over in my hands. It was a plain, letter-sized envelope, fairly thick, with just my name written on the outside. "I don't know."

I almost tossed it inside so I could check it out later, when I wasn't on my way to kill vamps, but curiosity got the better of me. Although it bore only my first name in block capital letters, I thought I recognized the handwriting as Nick's. Still standing in the doorway, I tore open the envelope.

Burning with curiosity, Robbie tried to read over my shoulder. "Who's it from? What's it say?"

The envelope bore several pages, all written in Nick's neat scribble. Just to make sure, I checked the signature. "It's a note from Nick."

"A note is a few words," Robbie said, craning his neck for a better view. "That's a full-blown letter. An actual letter. No one writes letters anymore. They send texts or e-mails. If someone writes a letter, it's because it's really important, like they've decided to go off to Borneo or kill themselves or become a Mormon. What's it say?"

I read a few lines, mainly to satisfy myself that Nick wasn't planning on committing suicide or something equally stupid. Seeing that wasn't the case, I quickly folded the sheets and returned them to the envelope. I'd read enough to know it wasn't something to be read in the doorway with Robbie hovering around. "Nothing horrible," I said. "I'll read it later."

"It's got to be important, though," Robbie protested. "People don't write casual letters and tape them to your door."

"It's about his feelings on being able to see ghosts. I think he just had to write it out to sort out his mind. But he's fine. I'll read it later. I've got to get going."

I hadn't lied to Robbie. From the few sentences I'd read, part of the letter was indeed about Nick's reactions to seeing ghosts. But I'd also caught some other parts of the missive that made my heart lurch. I knew I couldn't read Nick's words with Robbie present, so I loaded my gear into Gina's car and drove a few blocks away and parked. I got the letter back out and read it carefully.

I read quickly at first. After all, I had vamps to kill. But after a few lines, I forgot about the traffic rushing by my car and the setting sun, and pretty much everything except for Nick.

It read:

> *Dear Duncan,*
>
> *I have to write and get this down on paper, mainly so that I can marshal my thoughts and get things straight in my head, but also to let you know what I truly feel. I can't really say these things to your face, not without copious amounts of alcohol, anyway. And an e-mail is much too impersonal. Plus, I just like writing things out by hand. Makes me concentrate more.*
>
> *First, I think I'll tell you about my date last night. It's really the catalyst that made me need to get this off my chest, so I'll give you all the gritty details. Such as they are.*
>
> *The guy's name is Brandon, not that it's important. He's a really nice guy, or at least he seems*

to be. And under other circumstances, he might have been good for me. He's thirty, kind of hot, and a teacher as well, although at a different school from mine. In a weird way, he reminds me of you in that he's a bigger guy, obviously works out, and seems to have a good sense of humor, although I may have taxed his kindness as the night went on. Actually, I know I did.

We decided we'd have a traditional sort of first date: dinner and a movie. We never made it to the movie. Too bad, because they say Denzel Washington is really good in it. But I digress. We ate downtown at the Churchill. I got there first and got a table for us and waited. While I was there, taking in my surroundings, I realized that there was a spirit standing behind the bar. He was a younger guy, maybe in his midtwenties, and, even though my nerves were telling me something was amiss, at first I thought he was just one of the bartenders. But then one of the living bartenders walked right through the guy, so I knew he was a ghost. And what's more, this spirit knew I was watching him. He knew I could see him, and I think he could see I was a little nervous. I was, both because I was anxious about my date, who was due to arrive at any second, and because I just didn't expect to see some ghost at the Churchill, acting as if he still worked there. You'd think I'd be used to seeing them pretty much anywhere by now, but I think I was concentrating on my date so much that he caught me off guard. Anyway, when he saw that I not only could see him but that he had shocked me, he got this huge grin on his face.

Brandon arrived just then, so I turned and tried to ignore the ghost as best I could. If Brandon noticed that my palms were sweating and that I couldn't seem to talk without stumbling over words, he didn't let on. Maybe he just took it as first date jitters. The spirit, though, came around the bar and joined us, standing right behind Brandon as he sat down. I tried my best to keep my eyes on Brandon's face as we talked, but I know every now and then I was glancing up at the ghost. And the ghost, I might add, was enjoying himself immensely. I've heard about mischievous spirits before, but this was my first encounter with one. He did everything to throw me off. He mimicked Brandon's movements. He even sat down at our table and sat there with a gleam in his eyes, watching intently as Brandon would ask me a question, and then shift his gaze to me when I answered. Things like that.

The waiter brought our food, and I thought maybe the ghost had had his fun and was going to let us alone. He got up from the table and acted as if he was walking away, but suddenly he was right behind me, his face right up to my ear. "He's nice," he said. "First date?"

I nearly answered him! Luckily I caught myself in time and went on talking to Brandon. I'm sure my increasing nervousness was beginning to annoy my date a little. He kept asking if I was okay. "You keep looking off to the side. Someone here you know?" Things like that. I figured if I told him I was being bothered by a pesky ghost, that would end the date right then and there, so I tried to carry on.

After a few minutes, I think I was getting pretty good at not paying our unwelcome friend any attention. I had to bite my tongue several times, but I managed. The spirit, realizing that he wasn't getting under my skin anymore, decided to escalate things. He sat back down and looked from Brandon to me. I could tell he was sucking in energy. The air was getting that chill, a feeling with which I'd become all too familiar. Even Brandon noted the drop in temperature. With a grin, the ghost shot his hand out so that it hit

Brandon's wine glass. I saw it start to topple and quickly reached out and grabbed it before it soaked both the tablecloth and Brandon's lap. Brandon thanked me, saying I'd made a nice catch and that he couldn't figure out how the glass had started to tip in the first place, and he hadn't felt the table move or anything. I made some remark about hitting the bottom of the table with my knee as I crossed my legs, although I hadn't. The ghost wasn't finished, though. He'd found an audience to his shenanigans, and he wasn't going to let the opportunity go to waste.

He looked again at Brandon. "Got yourself quite a hunk there, Sparky," he said. He'd called me Sparky since he sat down. I don't know why, other than to annoy me. "Going to let him bone you tonight?"

I know I shouldn't have, but I told him to go away. I said it through clenched teeth and low, but Brandon still heard me.

"Pardon?" he asked.

I told him it was a muscle cramp that I was telling to go away. It seemed more sane than revealing I was talking to a ghost. The spirit then asked me again if I was planning on ending the evening with sex. He looked at me doubtfully. "You're not, are you? I can tell. You like the guy, but not enough." Something along those lines, anyway. Then he grinned. "So, you don't mind if I get some action, do you?" And then he disappeared beneath the table. Then I heard him making slurping noises and I could see the top of his head periodically as he bobbed up and down over Brandon's lap. I knew he wasn't really doing anything, but I'm afraid my temper burst at that point and I suddenly stood up and shouted, "Would you just leave us the fuck alone?" Needless to say, I shocked not only Brandon, but also the rest of the patrons at the

Churchill, including a family at a table right next to us with three young kids.

That pretty much ended the date. I tried to explain to Brandon what had occurred, but I'm pretty sure that he'd already labeled me as a lunatic and begged off the rest of the evening, saying he didn't think we were well suited and that he thought we should just call it off then and not protract the inevitable. I felt like an ass. I didn't feel any better as, when Brandon was making a hasty exit, the spirit looked at him and muttered, "What an ass!"

I was pretty pissed off last night, but this morning I guess I'm thankful that the ghost, whose name I never did get—nor did I bother, after all the fracas was all over, to find out if he wanted to move on or not—and I'm pretty sure the answer would have been negative anyway, as he was having too much fun—, because he made me realize some things. (I just looked at the preceding sentence, and it's a good thing I'm a history teacher and don't teach English!) Anyway, I think a lot of this I knew, deep down, but wasn't ready to admit. But now that I'm thinking it, I have to tell you. I'm just not brave enough to do it face to face.

You know how I feel about you. We don't talk about it much, I know, but my feelings haven't changed. I also know that you and Robbie are probably more committed to each other now more than ever. And I've come to accept that. I thought I was resigned to be your friend and nothing more, and I was okay with that. At least, I thought I was. But lately I've been feeling like you and I have drifted apart even as friends. I guess I feel like the outsider. I mean, you've got Robbie, Gina, and even Daisy. And then there's me. Just a regular guy, who really didn't belong in your little group. And I seemed to be left out of so much.

So if I'm being honest, that's why I made my request to Gina. I couldn't bear to not be part of the group.

The ghost at the Churchill made me realize something else, though. I don't want to date someone else. I know I shouldn't wait for you. After all, it's obvious that you and Robbie are going to be together for the long run. In the back of my mind, I guess I thought that at some point Robbie would move on and you'd be free. Maybe you and I would start dating or maybe we wouldn't, but at least I'd have a chance. After all, when we first met, you thought yourself that you needed human companionship. But it's been quite a while now, and I know that isn't going to happen. You two are too attached.

I'm still glad I did what I did. With the ghosts, I mean. Despite last night, I think I can do some good, and maybe even help you out every now and then. I'm no longer the useless human in the group. Part of me says that I should make a clean break from you guys, that I won't move on (dating-wise) while you're in my life. And I gave that serious consideration. But I can't. I want to be around you, even if there's no chance of us ever getting together.

So the ball is in your court. You know how I feel, but I never seem to know how you feel. You play things close to your chest. If you feel uncomfortable with me hanging around, knowing how I feel about you, I understand completely. And I'll stay away. But I hope you'll still want me as a friend, if nothing else. It's your call.

Love,

Nick

P.S. I'll probably be too chicken to hand this to you, so I'll probably leave it on your car or door or *something. I feel a bit foolish writing all this, but I thought I needed to make my statement before I talked myself out of it.*

I stuffed the pages back into the envelope and restarted the car. Pulling into traffic, I realized my jaw was clenched tightly and forced myself to relax a little. Poor Nick. And for that matter, poor me. Oh hell, throw in poor Robbie as well. We were all in a screwy situation, and I wasn't sure there would be a good outcome. I loved Robbie, but I couldn't help but think how things would be with Nick. Someone I could hold. Someone I could kiss. Someone I could—well, you know.

I headed toward the abandoned house, feeling pretty pissed at myself at how I was affecting those around me.

CHAPTER 10

IDEALLY, it's better to find a vampire while he or she is sleeping and stake their ass then. No muss, no fuss, and you're home in time for dinner. There is, however, something to be said for hunting them down when they're up and fighting, especially when you're in a crappy mood. And my mood could hardly have been crappier. I was only sorry I didn't have a werewolf and a few demons to hunt down as well. Throw in a zombie or a malevolent spirit, and my night would have been complete. Hell, the way I was feeling, I'd have ganked the Abominable Snowman from *Rudolph the Red-Nosed Reindeer. After* he had his teeth removed and was all nice and everything.

My only worry was that, by the time I got to the house Jennifer Peters' aunt owned, it was already well after dark, and the vamps might have gone out for the night, feeding on the innocent. It wasn't the sort of house one would want to hang around.

I didn't worry about parking away from the house and trying to sneak up on them. Vamps wake hungry, and they'd smell my blood, so performing a Pearl Harbor was out of the question. Instead I pulled up as close as I could to the door, and had my crossbow loaded and ready when I stepped out of the car. My duffel bag I slung over my shoulder.

The front door wasn't locked, so maybe they *had* already vamoosed for the night. If that was the case, Plan B was to torch the place. If I couldn't kill them, at least I was going to piss them off.

I turned the knob with my right hand and kicked out at the same time. The door swung and banged against the inside wall, making one hell of a noise.

"Lucy!" I shouted in my best Ricky Ricardo. "I'm home!"

The sudden breeze caused by my bashing in the door resulted in a large dust bunny skittering down the hall. I was so geared up that I nearly put an arrow through it. Luckily, I stopped myself in time. Being known as a private detective who's good at killing vamps was one thing. A private detective who's known as a badass dust-bunny killer didn't have quite the same ring to it.

I walked in a few paces. My senses were telling me the house was occupied. It was silent, but not the kind of silent you get with an empty house. At least one of the vamps was present. The hairs on the back of my neck were tingling.

I'm not sure if I actually heard movement from the kitchen area, or if my Spidey sense just kicked into gear, but I wasn't surprised when I saw a shadow fill the doorway. I heard a female voice say, "You've *got* to be kidding me." Then the shadow shifted as Kissy walked forward. She leaned against the doorframe, her body language oozing disdain. She obviously practiced boredom and smarm in equal doses.

There was enough light coming in from the kitchen windows that I could make out her features, but I was in the darkened hall. I doubt she had a good view of me. I was probably just a good-looking hunky shape in her hall. Even with her enhanced vision, she obviously hadn't registered that I was toting a crossbow. If she had, she was carrying the bored act a little far.

"I don't remember ordering delivery," she said, in a tone that was supposed to be mocking but wasn't working for me, "but I'm glad the food has arrived."

That's the trouble with vamps. They think nothing can harm them. No one believes they exist, so they're used to going around getting their own way. No Carl Kolchak to pound stakes in their hearts, no Buffy Summers to kick the crap out of them before destroying them, and no Sam and Dean Winchester to snuff them while being snarky with each other. You'd think someone bursting into the house and shouting would be a warning signal, but not to

Ms. Peters. She was lounging against the doorjamb with a finger to her lips, thinking she was in control of the situation.

"Stupid bitch," I said as I fired.

Vamps are fast, but not faster than an arrow being propelled from a crossbow. I saw her eyes flash as she realized what was happening. The fear was etched in her baby blues as the arrow pierced her chest. She screamed as she fell back, her hands automatically coming up, much too late, to try to ward off the blow. The scream died from her lips before she even hit the floor. I quickly flung the duffel bag off my shoulder and retrieved another arrow. I reloaded the crossbow before cautiously approaching her body. She wasn't moving, but I was still getting danger vibes, so I wanted to be careful.

Jennifer "Kissy" Peters wouldn't be chomping on any more necks. She was as dead as the proverbial doorknocker. She had fallen so that her face was right in the path of a moonbeam, making her pale skin almost translucent. Her eyes were open, as was her mouth. I could tell my arrow had hit its mark without getting too close. There wasn't much blood around the arrow sticking out of her ribcage, slightly to the left of center. More was coming out of her mouth, actually, dribbling down her chin onto her throat. The wooden shaft of the arrow was firmly embedded. It had been a good shot. Granted, she had been only several yards away, but you try hitting someone smack dab in the heart in a darkened house. Not easy, unless you're as good as me. Just sayin'.

I was just about to turn back to the hallway when I found out why the red flashing lights in my head hadn't ceased. With an enraged snarl, someone jumped onto my back, making me drop the crossbow. I knew without being able to see him that it was Braedon Isaacs and not Dominic Hunt. This was definitely a short guy, as his feet didn't hit the ground with his arms hoisted up on my shoulders. I could feel his hot breath as he tried to sink his teeth into me. I twisted, trying to buck him off, but he was strong. Arnold Schwarzenegger strong. His screech was filled with anger and lust and hunger, and I knew instinctively that his fangs were much too close to the soft skin of my neck.

Not being able to throw him off, I threw myself sideways. The two of us crashed into the wall, but he took the brunt of the blow. One of his arms was reaching around my chest and the other was on my head, trying to force me to turn it so that he could chow down. The collision with the wall didn't make him lose his grip, but it did make him pause, and gave me a few seconds to avoid getting bitten. I took advantage of the time by slamming him against the wall again. The second go didn't have quite the force of the first, but it did the trick. He almost fell off my back on his own. I bent over and shoved myself forward, which resulted in his head bashing against the wall. He slumped off, falling onto his back.

It was, as I'd assumed, Braedon. He was wearing jeans and a white dress shirt stained with blood. I assumed the blood wasn't his. I wasn't bleeding, so the little drummer boy must have already had a snack and had been a messy eater. Lying there with a trickle of blood around his lips, he looked even smaller than when I'd seen him in the alleyway. His size wouldn't have been worrying if he'd been human, but he had vamp strength going for him, especially if he'd just fed. And vamps don't run out of energy easily. In a fight, I was definitely at a disadvantage.

Still bent over, I tried to pick up my crossbow, but Braedon recovered too quickly and he reached out and grabbed me by the ankle. He snarled and pulled and twisted, throwing me off balance. I fell, hitting a shelf on my way down to the floor and sending some glass and crockery crashing to the ground, where it shattered with one hell of a din. One might be tempted to say it was loud enough to wake the dead, but as one of the dead was already up and trying to kill me, the point was moot.

I hit the ground hard, but I managed to get my arms in front of me so my elbows absorbed most of the shock as I crashed to the floor. With more hissing, he practically crawled up my prone body and tried once again to get at my throat. I attempted to twist around so that we were face to face, but the little fucker was both strong and determined. We wrestled around, and I managed to maneuver us so I could get my left palm against his chin. I pushed his face back, at least keeping his slimy teeth away from my neck. One of his hands went to my throat, and I thought at first he was going to try to throttle me. Maybe he thought so too, but then he decided to try to force my hand off his chin.

Bad move on his part, because if he'd gone ahead with trying to strangle me, I'm not sure I'd have had the strength to stop him. As it was, while he was trying to pry my left hand from his chin, I was trying to get my flask out of my hip pocket with my right hand. I succeeded, and flipped off the cap just as he forced my hand off his face. He grinned triumphantly, and a fleck of saliva spattered out and nearly got me in the eye as he bent his head forward, his fangs making a beeline for my jugular. I shot my arm up, splashing some of the contents of the flask onto his face.

He shrieked and screamed something at me I didn't quite get, but I think it was a slur about my parentage. His hands immediately covered his face, which was smoking like coals that had just been doused with water. With Braedon being more concerned with his face bubbling with nasty-looking sores, it was easy to kick the little bastard off me. He fell back, still screaming and calling me some not very creative names as I made a grab for the crossbow. Unfortunately, I had to load the arrow back into place, and lost precious seconds. By the time I was ready and spun around to fire, he had recovered somewhat. He was a fast bugger, I'll give him that.

I was trying to get a bead on his heart when he leaped right over me and bounded toward the window. He jumped, his hands still protecting his face, and went right through. The glass shattered and would have cut a human to ribbons, but Braedon had an advantage—any cuts he received wouldn't bleed much, as he didn't have that much blood in him in the first place, and the wounds would heal quickly. Quicker, once he fed again.

I scrambled to my feet and went after him, although I chose the door, as I didn't want to get humongous cuts all over my body by diving out the window and encountering the shards of glass still in place. That, and I'm just not a leaper.

I threw open the door and saw that he was heading across the yard toward the sharp incline. His screams echoed in the night air, and I'm pretty sure he was simply running blind, as his hands were covering his face. I raised the crossbow and fired.

He was too far away and it was too dark to get a really good shot, but I hit him in the back. Braedon had just gotten to the top of the incline as the arrow struck home, and the force of the blow sent him flying. A more guttural scream escaped his lips as he disappeared from my sight. I heard a loud crash as he hit bottom, and I started to run across the yard to finish the job. I knew the arrow hadn't pierced his heart. I couldn't be sure, but it looked like I'd hit his right side instead of his left. Still, with the holy water, the dive through the window, and now an arrow in his back, I was guessing old Braedon wasn't feeling all that tip-top.

I got to the crest of the hill and looked down. Braedon had fallen right on top of the picket fence surrounding the neighboring house. I could see him in the moonlight, squirming on the ground as if he were trying to get up. The moon gave his skin a pale glow, accentuating the blood that was gushing from his mouth and from a wound in his side. His shirt, nearly glowing blue in the moonlight, was rapidly getting darker from the piece of wood that had pierced his side. He must have hit the fence hard, as he'd taken out about seven planks on impact. Littered about his flailing body were shards of wood of various sizes. The one sticking out of his abdomen was about the size of a toddler's arm.

I didn't have to hurry to get down to him. He wasn't going anywhere. I picked my way carefully, as I didn't want to trip over some hidden tree root or something and take a gainer down the hill. That would have lost me massive cool points. Still, in a minute or two I was standing over Braedon, looking down at him. His face looked like a bubbling pepperoni pizza. Well, an oozing, bubbling pepperoni pizza. I suddenly realized I was hungry, but a trip to Pizza Hut on the way home was definitely *not* on the agenda.

A gurgling sound erupted from his throat as more blood gushed out. His eyes, already becoming glassy, realized someone was near him. He looked at me and attempted a smile. His hands were feebly trying to pry the wood out of his side. The arrow must have broken off upon landing. It hadn't gone all the way through, as I could see no exit wound on his chest, so part of it was still imbedded in him. Good.

"You missed," he hissed at me.

I reached over and picked up part of one of the shattered pieces of wood. It was nice and pointy. "Not this time," I said as I plunged it into his chest. He screamed and tried to get his hands up to try to ward off the blow, but he was too weak. The scream turned into a gasp and then a whimper as Braedon Isaacs died for a second time. His hands dropped and his head slumped to the side. Off in the distance, I heard the hoot of an owl.

Three down. One to go.

CHAPTER 11

I RETURNED to the house, hoping to find Dominic Hunt there. I was pretty worn out, but it would be nice to get him out of the way so I could get back to my life and convincing Robbie to stick around, and then figuring out what to do with Nick. Searching the place, I not only didn't find him, but I didn't even get a sense of him there. Maybe he had his own little hidey-hole, preferring not to room with the Bobbsey Twins. I stuck around for another hour or so, though, thinking he might show up. Assuming Hunt had turned Kissy and Braedon into vamps, he would have known instinctively that they had been destroyed. I wandered from room to room, but nothing. I decided it was time for a good night's sleep, so I gathered up my stuff and started out to the car.

As soon as I stepped out of the front door, I should have realized I wasn't alone. Maybe I was just too tired, but my psychic sense that alerted me whenever the spooky-ookies were around didn't go off. Maybe it was taking a vacation. Either way, I'd walked several yards before I realized someone was standing by my car. The moon was behind him, so all I could see was a tall shape with long hair, wearing a long coat. Dominic Hunt.

He was just standing there, seemingly calm. If he was pissed off because I'd killed his two pals, he didn't show it. I stopped in my tracks, wondering how quickly I could load up one of the crossbows. Not fast enough. I dropped the duffel bag onto the ground so I wouldn't be encumbered if I had to fight or take flight. I kept my right hand near my hip pocket, where my flask was still nestled, half-full of holy water.

"You've been busy," Hunt said, his voice calm. Too calm. It was almost melodic.

I smiled. I'm not sure he could see it, but it comforted me anyway. When confronted by a man-eating tiger, it's best not to let the tiger know you want to piss your pants. "All in a night's work," I said. I'm pretty sure my voice didn't shake. Almost sure. My fingers inched closer to the flask.

"Braedon and Kissy?" He posed it as a question, but not one he expected an answer to.

Why wasn't he attacking? Did he really want to have a good heart-to-heart chat before we tried to kill each other? "You'll have to find new friends," I said.

Hunt took a step forward. I could barely make out his lips, which were gently smiling. "Maybe you could be that new friend."

"Not likely."

He took another step toward me. "Think before you turn me down so quickly. I sense dissatisfaction in you. You are one not happy with your life."

"Says you." Me, not happy? I had a dead boyfriend who was still around whom I couldn't have sex with and, a dog that ate squirrels to keep her undead existence going, and a very nice history teacher whose life I was wrecking. What was there to be unhappy about?

"Ah, but I can see through you," Hunt said. Another step. He was now too close for comfort. "You fight against my kind without truly understanding what we can offer you. What I can offer you."

"Yeah?" My hand was on the flask. "What's that?"

His grin broadened. "Love. Love that will never die."

Cap off. Ready to throw. Take another step, asshole. Get a face full of the good stuff.

Maybe he was really good at reading body language and knew what I had in mind. In any case, he stopped moving. He seemed to be taking me in, every detail. There was a glint in his eyes, as if he liked what he saw. I don't know if he found me good-looking or just saw me as a walking bag of blood. He chuckled. "Throw your holy water, if you want. You can't kill me."

"No?"

He shook his head. "I'm much too old. And much too fast."

It wasn't an empty boast. I had the flask out of my pocket and was splashing out some of the contents, but he was no longer there. He lunged and ducked so that the liquid flew right over him and splattered onto the ground. All I saw was his long dark hair billowing behind him as he threw himself at me. It was like being hit with a wrecking ball. We hit the ground with him on top of me. I did my best to ignore the pain that shot up through my back on impact and the air being knocked right out of me, but that's a lot to ignore. Hunt was maybe an inch or two shorter than me and probably matched my weight, but he had vamp strength going for him. I tried to wrestle him off me, but failed to budge him. His fangs were bared, and getting closer and closer to my neck. I managed to get my left hand up and onto his chin. I pressed as hard as I could, keeping his glistening teeth away from my skin, while my other hand felt the ground for the flask I'd dropped when he tackled me. I couldn't find it.

There was a triumphant gleam in his eyes. He knew I didn't have the strength to hold out for long. He grasped my wrist with fingers than felt like steel and forced me to relinquish my grip on his chin. With a low growl, he bent his head down and bit into my neck.

I know I winced. I may have even cried out. When someone is on top of you and has sunk his teeth into your throat, it's hard to concentrate on anything else. I know I didn't stop struggling, but my fighting him seemed to make him enjoy it all the more.

I'd read a lot about the sexual nature of a bite from a vampire, and it's undeniable that there's a salacious aspect to the act. I just wasn't prepared for just how sexual it was. At first, all I could think of was the feel of his fangs piecing my skin, and then his lips around the wound, sucking in the blood. I was vaguely aware of his erection that was pressing against my leg. I was repulsed and angry at myself for getting myself into the situation. If I hadn't been so arrogant that

I'd thought it would be an easy task to kill three vampires in one night, I might have avoided getting bitten. I should have been better prepared. I should have waited until Gina returned so that I had backup. I should have done anything other than what I did.

But in seconds, all those thoughts left my mind, and I was only aware of Dominic Hunt lying on top of me, his lips pressed to my throat. Part of me still wanted to push him off me and ram a stake right into his chest, but part of me was intrigued by the connection I felt with him. It was as if we were in the throes of ecstasy, two individuals becoming one through carnal lust. I realized I was hard as well, and I was no longer struggling. My arms were wrapped around his back. His were on my shoulders, and I could feel his weight and strength as he held me down.

He squirmed, and I think I may have gasped. I could feel his dick, long and hard, still pressing against my leg, almost as clearly as if we had been naked. I felt a tremble go through his body, and his cock pulsed as he climaxed. I felt his dick throbbing against me as he buried his face with even more force against my throat. Some strands of his long hair were against my face and I was acutely aware of his scent, patchouli mixed with a slightly sour smell reminiscent of old wood combined with sweat and blood.

After what seemed an eternity, he lifted his face. He was smiling, and some of my blood was still on his lips. My breathing was ragged, and it was all I could do to keep my eyes on him. I felt so weak that all I wanted to do was sleep for about a week, but I had to see what he would do next. He wouldn't want to turn me, I was sure, so I thought he would kill me to keep me from dying of his bite and returning as a vampire. I was sure he would reach up his strong hands and snap my neck or throttle me, but he rose slowly, his eyes never leaving mine. Looking down on me, he nodded.

"You are mine now, Duncan Andrews."

I wasn't sure if he spoke the words, or if they were just in my head. I reached up and touched my neck with my left hand. I could feel where his teeth had broken the skin, but the wounds were quickly healing. I could detect no blood on my throat. I closed my eyes briefly. When I opened them, Dominic Hunt was gone.

I don't know how long I lay there on the grass. It seemed like days, but it was probably only minutes. With great effort, I raised my head. The moon was still high in the sky, so not much time had passed. I looked around me, feeling woozy and disoriented. The flask I'd dropped was several feet away. I rolled onto my side, a movement that almost made me pass out. I took a few deep breaths before attempting to move again. Slowly, I reached out and grasped the flask. A lot of the contents had spilled out, but there was still a little of the precious liquid sloshing around inside.

I felt dozens of emotions all at once. I was angry at myself, not only for getting bitten, but also for the part of me that had felt connected with Hunt. I could barely get the image of his face out of my mind, and his words kept reverberating in my head. I was his now. I was his. And a weakness in me was not only okay with that, but it was thrilled by the idea.

I clenched my teeth together and growled out loud. That wasn't me. That was the vampire's victim talking. And I was no one's victim.

Crying out with the effort, I brought the flask up and splashed the rest of the holy water onto my neck where Hunt had sucked out some of my blood.

I knew that it would hurt, but I had no idea that there could be that much pain. The liquid hissed as it hit the bite marks, and I could smell burning flesh. I screamed, aware only of the pain and the thin column of smoke coming up off my neck. I knew I was about to pass out, but I had to do one more thing before oblivion set in. My eyes were clouding over as I fished my phone out of my pocket. I forced myself to press the number I called most often. I don't know if I even got the phone up to my face. Everything was going dark. I heard a familiar voice, but it seemed very far off. Like it was coming from another dimension.

"Duncan?" I could hear Gina's voice, oh so far away.

"I…." I slumped back, exhausted. "I need you."

Blackness overcame me.

I DREAMED. Or maybe hallucinated. I was aware that I was unconscious, and vaguely aware that I was lying on the grass. But I was also standing on a seashore, although the landscape was bleak and desolate. I was wearing a white shirt and white pants and was barefoot. It was an odd, very vivid dream, because I could feel the sand between my toes. My back was to the water, but I could hear the waves lapping behind me, a calming sound. I turned my head slightly. The water was blood red. The sun was on the horizon, the sky around it a kaleidoscope of crimson, magenta, gold, and nearly every other color I could think of. The beach seemed strangely familiar, but I couldn't figure out why. I hadn't been to a beach in over twenty years. Seagulls circled the air above me, their screeches nearly mimicking human speech. It seemed like they were welcoming me.

I turned back and scanned the landscape. Beyond the beach was a rocky area. There was no sign of civilization. I felt panic well up inside me as I remembered Dominic Hunt's teeth sinking into my flesh. Had I died? Where was I? Was it really a dream?

There were three people standing on the beach. The closest was Hunt, dressed all in black, maybe a dozen feet away from me. His long hair was blowing in the slight breeze. His T-shirt was tight and I could see his pectoral muscles straining against the material. He was smiling.

"Duncan," he said, his tone welcoming.

There were two figures behind him, and at first they were mere shadows, but now they were coalescing into very familiar shapes. To Hunt's left was Robbie, wearing jeans and a mesh football jersey. He was standing stock still, as if he were a statue. His eyes were alive, though, and there was a little touch of panic in them. When he saw me, the panic vanished and was replaced by sorrow.

On Hunt's right was Nick, wearing dark pants, a dark shirt, and a tan blazer. He also looked sad.

"I'm part of you, now, Duncan Andrews," Hunt said. When he spoke, I found it impossible to accept that there was anything else of importance in the universe except him. "As you are a part of me."

The figure of Robbie started to raise his hand, as if he was going to wave a hello to me. As his hand came up, though, he grew more and more faint. Finally, he vanished from sight. Hunt's eyes twinkled. "The ghost. The great love of your life. The life you never had. The life you never will have. An impossible love."

Nick started to open his mouth as if to speak, but before any words could come out, he disappeared as well.

"The teacher. A man you also have strong feelings for." Hunt shook his head slowly. "You love him, but won't even admit it to yourself. But I see within you, Duncan Andrews. I know how you truly feel."

Was this a dream, or thoughts being projected into my head by Hunt? After all, my blood was part of him now. The bond between vampire and victim was strong. I'd always heard that, but experiencing it was something new.

Hunt's smile broadened, and I had the uncanny feeling he knew what I was thinking. "Two men. One you can't have because he's a mere vapor, a wraith, and the other you won't have because of your sense of honor and the love you feel for the first." He raised his hands, palms upward. "And then there's me. I offer you an eternity of love. You and I could be gods."

My neck was tingling where I'd splashed it with holy water. Maybe that act had lessened the hold Hunt had over me. I took a deep breath, gathering in strength. Exhaling slowly, I shook my head. "Not going to happen."

"You're strong," Hunt said. "But you know that I'll win in the end."

Go to him, something was telling me. *Let him embrace you. Feel his warmth, his strength. Feel his arms around you.*

I shook my head again, clearing it. I flashed Hunt a smile of my own. "I'm going to put a stake right through your black heart."

His smile faltered just for a second. "You know I'm right. You have no life with those other men. With me, you can have it all."

Suddenly, a howling wind kicked up, making Hunt's hair whip into his face. Even though it was partially obscured, I could see the gale wasn't something he'd expected. In the distance, lightning flashed, soon followed by a roll of thunder. Another bolt of lightning lit up the sky, and Hunt's smile vanished as he searched the horizon, trying to discern why his dreamscape was falling to pieces. The wind was kicking up sand and even drowning out the sound of the waves. Obviously, Hunt had no idea what was happening. My clothes were flapping as gust of wind whipped around me.

"That," I told him, "is the power of a witch. And between us, we'll destroy you."

I knew, because in the wind there could be heard a soft laughter. It was Gina's laugh.

I AWOKE, briefly, sometime around dawn. How I knew it was dawn wasn't entirely clear, because my eyes never made it all the way open. There was sunlight on my eyelids, though, and when I moved my hands a little, I felt dew on the grass. I shivered. I was feverish and weak. My throat felt like it was on fire, as did my head. I gave up on opening my eyes and tried to remember if I'd actually managed to call someone. Then I remembered the vision I'd had, with Dominic Hunt and the beach and the red tide and the wind and Gina's presence, invisible but strong. I may not have called 911, but I got hold of someone even better.

I think I groaned and then sank back into oblivion.

WHEN I opened my eyes the next time, the sun was high in the sky and a wet tongue was licking my cheek. Dark shapes were standing over me. I blinked, and the shapes formed into people. One was standing tall, looking down with mild concern on his face. Lieutenant Carson. The other was kneeling by my side, with massive concern on her face. Gina. The small tongue belonged to Daisy, who was doing her bit by soaking my cheek. There was another person behind Gina and Carson, and it took me a moment to figure out who it was. Mark the Dentist.

"I'm dreaming," I said.

Well, that's what I attempted to say. It came out "aww rerr rerr" even to my own ears. I cleared my throat and tried again. The second try didn't succeed much better. I tried to move, but Gina placed a hand on my chest.

"You've been laying here for hours," she said, a warning in her voice. Gently, she helped me raise my head off the ground. "I need you to drink this."

She had a little plastic cup in her hand, the kind you get with a bottle of nighttime cold medicine. This little cup wasn't filled with NyQuil, though, but some brown liquid that had black flecks swimming around in it. Gina was holding it right under my nose, and I got a whiff of the stuff. It smelled like puke mixed with cheddar cheese. I winced.

"You've got to be kidding," I muttered. Some of the words, this time, actually came out correctly.

"Drink it." Gina was insistent, so I drank. It didn't taste any better than it looked or smelled. I coughed. The sound made Daisy back up a few paces, and she eyed me warily. Maybe she thought I was about to spew something, and she didn't want to get hit by the spray.

Whatever potion had been in the cup was potent. In moments, my brain no longer felt like it was being barbequed. I still felt weak, but no longer felt like I should be being fitted with a halo and wings.

"What's in that stuff, besides turpentine and Tim Tebow's jockstrap?" I managed to sit up further, bracing myself on my elbows.

Gina smiled gently. "My special recipe. Ginger, nutmeg, cod liver oil, eye of newt, and crushed up Bayer aspirin."

Both Mark the Dentist and Carson frowned, not sure if she was joking or not. I twitched my left eye, the closest I could come to a wink, at Gina and tried to smile. "You should market that stuff. Get Tom Cruise to do your commercials. People already think he's crazy. Advertising witch's brews aren't that big a stretch for him." I started to get up, but failed somewhere along the point where your body is supposed to rise rather than fall back to the ground.

Gina told Carson and her boyfriend to help me to the car. They got me inside the back seat of a Cadillac I didn't recognize. It must have been Mark the Dentist's. Once inside and laying across the seat, I felt very sleepy. I heard someone close the car door behind me and then fell asleep, not waking until we got to my apartment. Even then I was groggy, and was aware mainly of leaning heavily against Mark as we marched down the hall to my place. Gina produced her key, and Mark led me inside. I suddenly realized Carson was no longer with us, and I may have even asked about him. Gina said something about him having to get back to work, and then I forgot everything because Robbie materialized before me, wearing cutoff jeans, basketball shoes, a tank top, and a worried look.

"I got him," he told Mark the Dentist.

And he did. I could feel his arms around me, helping me down the hall to our bedroom. Amazing how much energy worry and sheer terror can give a ghost. Robbie got me to the bed, where I plopped down and once again slept.

"YOU were inches from death," Gina said.

"Felt like centimeters."

I was still in bed. I'd slept, on and off, the rest of the day. Every time I woke up, Robbie was there, watching over me. Mark the Dentist had gone home, but Gina stayed, giving me potions every few hours and applying salves to my neck. I got the story in bits and pieces. I'd called Gina around midnight—it had seemed much later!—and she and Mark immediately packed up their stuff. Gina managed to get them booked on the first nonstop flight to Indianapolis in the morning, and had landed in the Circle City just after ten o'clock. Gina hadn't known what the emergency was, so she hadn't been sure if she should call the cops or not. She got in touch with Nick, who couldn't tell her anything. She contacted Lieutenant Carson, who thought he might know where I was. They met up, he'd driven them out, and the rest was history. Except....

"You stopped to pick up Daisy?" I asked. I wasn't angry, but it did seem an unnecessary step when I was lying there staring up at a black-robed dude with a scythe who was waiting to play chess with me.

"We met up here. She wanted to come along. End of story." Gina was leaning over the bed, daubing the wounds on my neck—which had almost entirely healed—with some concoction of hers. "Doused this with holy water, huh?"

"Seemed like the thing to do at the time."

"Saved you from becoming a vampire's bitch," she said, not unkindly. "What the hell were you thinking, trying to kill three at once?"

"Hey, I got two of them."

"And the third got you."

"True."

Robbie, who had been in bed with me every time I'd woken up and was now spooned up next to me, gently punched me in the side. I wasn't sure if ghost hits counted, as this one went right through me and all I felt was a chill. "Dumbass," he said. "I wish you'd get it into your head that you're not indestructible. You don't have no red S on your chest."

"Ungrammatical, but true." I was sitting up against the headboard and feeling better, although I wasn't planning on signing up for any marathons in the near future. Sniffing, I suddenly realized I was famished. I'd had potions and broths by the score supplied to me by Gina, but actual food was now definitely a priority. "I smell something cooking."

"Nick's making you supper." Gina got out some new concoction and stuck a cotton swab into the tiny bottle. The stuff was thick and gloppy. She applied some to my neck. It stung just a little, but being a big boy, I didn't wince. I just batted her hand away. She laughed and set the bottle on my nightstand. Apparently she'd smeared enough of it on me, because she didn't protest.

"When did he get here?" I had to fight the temptation to wipe the stuff off my neck. I'm pretty sure it was sizzling.

Robbie answered. "A little while ago. You were asleep."

Nick came in moments later, bearing a tray. He was all smiles as he set it down on my lap and helped me get situated into an eating-in-bed position. I stared at the food.

"Spaghetti?" It smelled fantastic, but then, I'd have eaten fried woodchuck if it had been put in front of me. "I'll get sauce all over my jammies." Not that I was wearing jammies. I had on a pair of worn sweats and no shirt, although I couldn't remember changing out of my clothes.

Nick grinned. "It's about all I'm capable of making. I'm not a cook."

Luckily, few people can ruin spaghetti. I tried a forkful. "It's delicious." I ignored the little splatter of sauce that hit my chest.

Gina had been rummaging in her black bag that she often carried, which contained her most-used potions and charms. She frowned. "I guess I'll have to go home for a bit. I won't be long, although I may have to do a bit of brewing, so to speak. No cauldron involved, though. I use the stove." Nick had raised an eyebrow at "brewing," so she added the rest for his benefit.

"What for? I'm feeling nearly human again." Especially with Nick's spaghetti filling my stomach. I swallowed and pointed my fork at him, and then at the plate. "Good sauce."

"It's Ragu," he admitted sheepishly.

Well, when you haven't eaten for ages, your taste buds are excited by nearly anything. Nick was obviously embarrassed to be in the room with me, and avoided looking in my direction. After making sure I could get the food up to my mouth easily, he moved back, keeping Gina in between us. I wanted to tell him everything was all right and that he didn't need to feel uncomfortable, but I couldn't with Robbie and Gina present. I'd have to catch him alone, and soon, to let him know he was still welcome.

Gina waited until our little exchange was over before explaining, "I need to get you a little potion for your brain, basically. You started the curing process with the holy water, and my little tinctures and ointments have pretty much wiped out the effects of being bitten. It's almost like his nasty little teeth never touched you." She was sliding into her coat, and paused to smack me on the arm. Unlike Robbie's punch, I felt hers. "Idiot! Anyway, there may still be a slight psychic connection between you and this vampire, and I've got a recipe that will take care of that."

"Yeah, I think he sent me some messages last night." The vision I'd had of the beach was still vivid in my mind.

"We don't want you to be getting mental texts from him as soon as the sun goes down," Gina said, adjusting her coat around her neck. "You know, all that 'Come to me, my little bitch, so I can chew on your neck' stuff. Really, it's so Barnabas Collins. Vampires annoy the shit out of me."

"Wait a second," I said, a forkful of pasta halfway to my mouth. A thought was niggling in my head. "As it is, how much am I under his influence? I mean, if he calls me, am I going to be playing the part of Mina Harker in *Dracula*? 'Oh, suck my blood, you big strong man.' Or is it going to be just like getting Facebook messages to play games, annoying, but you can ignore them?"

Gina frowned, thinking it over. "I'd say your will is your own at this point. We just have to break the last link and you'll be totally free of him."

"But... leaving this link won't harm me."

Her frown deepened. "He might be able to know where you are, though. And you may still hear him calling you, if he does. The link is still there, but your will is your own. Mostly."

"Mostly?"

"It depends on how powerful a vampire he is. The older the vamp, the stronger the link. I'm pretty sure, though, that you're mostly you at this point. Maybe a tiny bit vamp bitch. This other potion will take care of that, though, and then he can call until his mental vocal chords are hoarse."

"Still, as it is, if he knows where I'm at, he'll come and I can put an arrow through his heart. Otherwise, we lose all track of him. It might take us days, even weeks to track him down. He's not going to go back to that house, unless he's a blithering moron, and he didn't strike me as a blithering moron."

Gina sat on the side of the bed. She shook her head. "I said there was still a psychic connection between the two of you, and I think it's just that. I could be wrong, though. You know how a victim yearns for another bite from the vampire? What if some of that is still buried deep within your brain? Say he comes after you, and suddenly that bond is strengthened? You might not be able to resist. Then he'd bite you again, and we'd be back here, or worse. He might drain your blood and, honestly, I'm not ready to deal with a vampire Duncan Andrews. The human one is difficult enough."

"I'm fine."

"It's too dangerous!"

Robbie was in agreement. "We'll track him down. There are other ways."

"But they take longer." I could be a stubborn cuss. "Really, I'm not feeling any connection with him at all. No desire to write 'Duncan and Dominic' inside valentine hearts all over my composition book."

Gina gritted her teeth in exasperation. "That's because it's daylight, numbnuts! He's off being dead and sleeping!"

Nick, who was hovering at the foot of the bed and trying to look like he understood everything we were talking about, piped up. "I've got to say that I agree with them, Duncan. Surely if there's any danger, it's best to be safe and knock out this psychic connection or whatever it is while we can."

"But danger—" I started.

"If you say something butch like 'Danger is my middle name,'" Robbie said, looking at me like he was scolding a bad dog, "I'm going to punch you in the nuts, and I swear that you'll feel it."

We went on arguing back and forth, but in the end, I let Gina go off and brew her little potion, mainly because all the talking was getting in the way of my eating, and the spaghetti was getting cold. Besides, she could brew all the potions she wanted. It didn't mean I'd have to take them.

I had a plan. And more than that, I wanted to destroy Dominic Hunt as quickly as possible. And if he suffered while I was killing him, so much the better. The vampire had made me feel violated and at someone's mercy.

And I hated feeling like that.

CHAPTER 12

"HOW are you feeling?" Nick asked.

"You know how when you oversleep, and you think you should feel like you've got extra energy, but instead you feel groggy and want to go back to bed to sleep off all the sleepiness? That's how I feel."

We were in the park. The sky was overcast and threatening rain, although all it had managed so far was a little mist. Not horrible weather, but enough to keep people from coming to the park, which wasn't a bad thing when you had a dog that hunted down squirrels to eat their brains. Robbie was with us, and he and Daisy had run off to a copse of trees where Daisy was busy hunting her prey. I couldn't see them, but I heard the crunch of bones followed by Robbie's voice, a mixture of praise for Daisy and disgust at what he was seeing. "Oooh. That was a good one! Sorry, Rocket J. Squirrel!" Gina, finally satisfied that I wasn't going to go all maidenish and swoon all over the place, had gone to spend the evening with Mark the Dentist. After all, they had cut their vacation short so she could come to my rescue.

I was wearing a tan trench coat and hoping I didn't look too much like Castiel from *Supernatural*. I was pretty sure I was too tall for anyone to mistake me for Columbo. Nick was all zipped up in a heavy black jacket, hands jammed into his pockets, but he still looked cold. Robbie, who didn't feel the chill in the air, was donning a favorite sleeveless shirt with Alice Cooper's mug emblazoned on it. Nick and I were ambling along slowly, for which I was grateful. I'd have hated to ask for a rest period.

Off to our left, a grinning Robbie emerged from behind a tree. He yelled our way, "You guys should have seen that one! It was gnarly!"

Gnarly. My boyfriend said things like gnarly. Although he'd been around in the ten years plus since he'd died, in many ways Robbie would always be twenty years old. He'd certainly always look twenty.

On the other hand, he was so happy, traipsing around with our dog—who had blood and brain matter currently dripping from her chops—and we'd been through so much together, how could I just give it all up? Especially as it seemed to be me who was keeping his spirit earthbound.

And Nick. Close to my age, devilishly good-looking, smart, and with a great sense of humor. And honorable. How many people would volunteer to open their minds so they could see ghosts in order to help them? So far we hadn't discussed the letter he'd left, but it was hanging in the air between us, so to speak, and couldn't be put off for too much longer.

Robbie took off again to the area beside the little creek that ran through the park, chasing Daisy, who in turn was bounding after a hapless squirrel. If it had been anyone else, I'd have said Robbie was getting some exercise in, but ghosts didn't need to work out. All he was doing was using up energy. He'd have to vanish for hours to recover from this little jaunt.

I glanced over at Nick, who was staring ahead at nothing. His eyes had a twinge of sadness to them. "How's the ghost seeing coming along?" I asked. "After all, Gina's back now. She can fix it so that you're back to normal if you like."

"Normal's overrated."

"You won't get any argument from me."

We stopped walking. Nick seemed to be looking across the street from the park at some of the houses there. A few of them were all decked out for Halloween. One had a few blow-up figures dotted around the lawn. Cute, nonthreatening ghosts and a plump vampire showing his fangs. The vampire was smiling pleasantly and resembled Count Chocula of cereal fame a little. I wanted to go over and stick a pin in him.

Nick shifted his head around, working some kinks out of his neck. "If you'd asked me a few days ago, I'd have jumped at the chance to have Gina work her mojo on me so that I wouldn't see them anymore. It seemed like they purposely were showing up at just the wrong times. I'd pull up at a stoplight, and one would pop up out of the ground right in front of my car, startling the shit out of me. Standing in line at Starbucks, I'd see one sitting in one of the booths. I mean, who the hell haunts a Starbucks?"

"Someone who never broke their caffeine addiction?"

Nick chuckled, shaking his head. "But... I don't know. I just feel that there's a reason I wanted to do this, one that I wasn't even aware of. Something is telling me that I'm doing the right thing, and whatever purpose it's supposed to be serving, I haven't done it yet. I know that doesn't make any sense, but I can't explain it. I just know I can't go back. It's like I know something is coming. It's just not here yet."

I patted his shoulder. My hand didn't seem to want to leave him, so I kept it there. "As long as you're not doing it to be like yours truly. The world doesn't need two of me."

"Hardly. Besides, I don't have your dress sense. I couldn't pull off the Bogart trench coat."

Damn. I hadn't even thought of him. "Bogart? Really? You're not getting a Castiel vibe? Bogart?"

"What's wrong with Humphrey Bogart?"

"He was a little guy and ugly as puss."

Nick nodded, not wanting to argue the point. "Good actor, though."

"Oh yeah, great actor. *Maltese Falcon.*"

"*Casablanca.*"

"And who could forget him in *The African Queen.*"

"I could," Nick said. "I've never seen it."

Another pat, and I removed my hand. The contact had been casual but oh so dangerous. Feeling a twinge of guilt, I looked back to where Robbie and Daisy were running circles around each other. If anyone other than me was disturbed by my having my arm around Nick, they weren't showing it. To make sure my hands didn't misbehave, I shoved them into my pockets. "I'll have to show it to you sometime," I muttered.

"Are you okay?" Nick touched my elbow. "I mean, I know you're still getting over a vampire attack, but you're looking a little pale. More so, I mean."

Truth was, I wasn't feeling too chipper. The sun going down probably had something to with it, since it meant my old buddy Dominic would be up and around, searching for blood. Maybe mine. I managed a weak smile. "I'm fine. Maybe we ought to be heading back, though."

We hadn't gone more than four paces, though, before I had to stop. I put a hand to my temple in an attempt to keep my brain from gushing out of my ears. Suddenly I had Excedrin Headache #422— throbbing cranium caused by vampire bite. I closed my eyes.

Red. My eyes were still closed but I could still see, at least with my mind's eye. The grass around us was red, the sky a deep crimson. Scarlet trees bore scarlet leaves. Even Nick was bathed in a red glow.

"Duncan." The voice I heard was in my head, loud and clear. Like my skull was a bell tower, and Dominic's voice was the ringing bell.

"Can you hear that?" I asked. I knew Nick couldn't, but I had to hear my own voice. Make sure I could still talk and be heard.

"Hear what?"

I opened my eyes slowly. The grass was green. Well, green with a liberal amount of brown mixed in. The trees looked like trees and not bleeding vegetation. Nick was Nick. My head, however, still felt like it was modeling clay and some kindergartener was pounding it flat against a table.

"Get me home," I said.

THAT night, I did everything I could to avoid sleep. Whenever I closed my eyes, I saw Dominic Hunt's face. Did I really find him attractive, or was it the fact that I'd been the victim of his bite that made me see him as the model on every single vampire romance novel I'd ever seen? Impossible to tell. I just knew that if Colton Yates had been there with me, I'd have apologized. I was going through hell, and I was semiprotected by Gina's administrations. What it must have been like for him, I couldn't imagine.

I was in bed with Robbie. Well, sort of. I was lying there staring at the ceiling. He was with me, although he wasn't visible. Conserving his energy, he was just a disembodied voice coming from the other side of the bed, a phenomena that can be disconcerting if you're not used to it.

"Something's bothering you," he said.

"I'm fine." After Nick had managed to get us all back to the apartment, he'd wanted to stay, but I convinced him it had just been a momentary lapse. He'd wanted to call Gina, but she was the last person I wanted to see at the moment. She'd make sure I took her potion, and I wasn't ready for that yet. It would be hard, but I had to keep the psychic connection with Hunt going a little longer. If I could.

"Oh yeah. You're fine. And there's a Nigerian prince who needs your banking information so that he can transfer his millions into the United States." I couldn't see Robbie, but I could imagine his arms crossed over his chest and his eyes doing a roll.

"Well, if I'm not fine," I said, "then surely what I need is sleep, which I can't get if you keep nattering on about how I'm not fine."

For a moment, all I could hear were Daisy's gentle snores as she rested by the foot of the bed. She didn't actually need to breathe, being a zombie and technically dead, and therefore snoring seemed to be a moot point, but I think she did it out of habit. To annoy me.

I found myself waiting for Robbie's next words. I knew he wasn't finished, that he had more to say, and I didn't blame him, as I was so obviously lying about being okay. Sure enough, he eventually spoke up. "Duncan?"

"Yeah?"

"You awake?"

"Nope. Fell asleep minutes ago."

Pause. "I know you always think you're doing the right thing. That you know what's best. I'm just not always sure you're right."

Was he still referring to getting bitten by Hunt, or about him passing over to the other side? Either way, the answer was the same. "I know what I'm doing."

"You didn't use the best judgment, though, going against three vamps. Sometimes I think you just blunder in and hope for the best."

"I'm good at blundering. Says so on my business cards."

There was a slight stirring in the air on his side of the bed, and then I could see him as he appeared, wearing his basketball shorts, curled up and looking over at me with concern. "What are you going to do when I go away?"

I closed my eyes. "I thought we weren't going to talk about that anymore."

"*You* said that. I didn't."

"Well, you're not going to go, so the question is already answered."

He reached over and stroked the side of my head. Well, his hand went through my ear, anyway.

"I just hope Nick looks after you."

Sighing heavily, I turned my head toward him. "Look, I like Nick. But I've got you. I don't need anyone else."

Robbie's smile was a sad one. "You need someone to look after you, you know. To keep you from being too much of a macho ass."

I frowned and then managed a smile of my own. "So that's how you see our relationship? That you look after me? Funny, I always thought it was the other way around."

"Yeah, you would," he said, chuckling.

I tried to grab his hand, but he wasn't solid enough. "So if I love you and you love me, why all this talk about moving on?"

"Because I know how difficult things are for you. We both know we can't go on like this forever, and you'll never agree to it, so it's up to me to make the decision."

Suddenly I was very tired. My idea about staying awake wasn't working, anyway. I was starting to see Hunt's face in the shadows beyond our bed. The lampshade over on Robbie's nightstand seemed to have grown a long head of hair, and now had eyes, a nose, and very, very red lips. A shadow by the closet seemed to be in human form and bore an uncanny resemblance to Hunt's silhouette. "I think I'm going to sleep now," I said, "but I want you to do something for me."

"Anything."

"If I get up during the night, make sure I'm really awake. And if I try to leave the apartment, stop me. I don't care how you do it, just don't let me leave."

I couldn't see his face, but I could hear the alarm in his voice. "Okay," he said. "Is it… the vampire?"

Robbie was right. I often blundered right in, as if I could do everything on my own. But I didn't have to, as I had him. "Yeah," I said. It felt like an admission of guilt, saying the word.

"Should I get Gina?"

"No, just watch me." I immediately relaxed. I knew without doubt now that I wouldn't wander out into the night, seeking out Dominic Hunt to become his Kibbles 'n Bits. Robbie would find a way to stop me, even if it meant summoning up enough energy to clobber me with a two-by-four. Of course, now I could almost feel the worry coming from his side of the bed, but that's what lovers are for, right? Scaring the piss out of them when you're acting irrationally.

I WAS going to assume the dream I had was all part of the vampire victim thing, and in no way representative of my normal subconscious.

At first, it was like any other dream in that it made no sense and was just full-on weird. I was walking through a forest. There were no leaves on the trees, and the night was clear and still. I was tracking something, but I couldn't remember what it was. My gun was in my hand. I was wearing a long leather coat, not the Bogart trench. Somewhere, up in one of the trees, an owl hooted.

There were sounds in front of me. My prey, desperately trying to get away. I increased my speed, something usually difficult at night in the woods, because you tend to trip over roots, fallen branches, or rocks, but in a dream it's strangely manageable. Now I could see a shape in front of me, dodging in between trees. I could even hear his ragged breathing.

I darted forward. The guy I was after realized I was close. I could hear the desperation in his huffing and puffing. He came to a clearing and paused to look back, never a wise thing to do when you're being chased.

It was Robbie.

He was obviously exhausted. Somehow I knew I'd been tracking him for quite a while, wearing him down, even though the dream had started right in the middle, so to speak. He tried to dash across the clearing, but knew he couldn't make it before I caught up with him. He stopped almost halfway through and looked back at me. He didn't look surprised or even angry or upset. Just resigned to his fate.

I strode into the clearing, gun raised. I knew what I was supposed to do, but somehow my finger wouldn't move against the trigger.

"Do it," Robbie said, sucking in air. "Get it over with."

The dream me had a stony face. The gun was aimed at the center of Robbie's chest. *Pull the trigger,* my mind was screaming. *You know you want to.*

But I didn't. I couldn't. I just stood there.

I felt hands on my shoulders as someone came up behind me, gripping me to give me encouragement. I knew without looking that it was Dominic Hunt. I felt his breath on my neck as he leaned in to whisper to me, "It's the only way."

"I can't," I said.

"You love him, I know, but you have to let him go. Pull the trigger." Hunt's voice seemed to ring in my head. I could feel the power of his fingers as they clutched onto my shoulders, and his long hair was brushing up against the side of my head.

"No."

Hunt's lips kissed my neck as he released my shoulders and wrapped his arms around me. "He's the dream. You have to let the dream go to allow reality to begin."

And the dream me pulled the trigger.

MERCIFULLY, the dream shifted at that point and I didn't see the bullet hit Robbie, although it wasn't necessary. In that way you know things in dreams, even if they aren't spelled out, I knew Robbie had been fatally shot. If he'd been alive and not a ghost, that is. But he had seemed made of flesh and blood as he'd bolted through the woods to his doom. Ghost or not, my pulling the trigger had felt like a betrayal.

Now, though, I was standing in my bedroom. Again, I *knew* it was my bedroom, even though it only bore a passing resemblance to it. For one, I rarely allowed so much fog to come into my apartment that it looked like every stick of furniture was floating on a cloud. I also didn't have red silk sheets on my bed. The window was spot-on, though. I'd give the dream that.

I was standing in my boxers, the bed in front of me. The covers were partially down and there was a red rose on my pillow. Someone standing behind me put their arms around my abdomen and kissed my neck. His long hair brushed my ear.

Dominic Hunt.

His hands caressed my stomach as his teeth nibbled at the tender skin of my throat. His fangs hadn't broken the skin, but were just scraping the surface. I shivered, telling myself it was because my neck had always been sensitive and that anyone playing the hickey monster would have produced the same result, and that it had nothing to do with Hunt himself, good-looking though he may have been. His hands seemed to be warming my torso as they roamed around.

Dream. This was a dream. Just wake up, dammit.

Not that that ever worked.

Worse, Hunt seemed to be inside my head, because he spoke softly into my ear. "You can't wake up. And I know that part of you doesn't want to."

He slowly turned me until we were facing each other. Like me, he was barely clothed, clad only in skimpy black briefs. The room was dim, but I could see his face plainly. The wide, sensuous mouth. The sparkling, slightly taunting eyes. He hugged me close to him, and I found my arms going around him as well. And then we kissed. I could feel his lips against mine and his tongue gently forcing its way into my mouth. Surely you didn't *feel* in a dream. The kiss became more passionate, and we were nearly crushing each other in our embrace.

Shit, shit, shit, double shit, and triple shit. My boxers were beginning to tent.

If your dream self punches your dream self's own face, does that wake you up? I couldn't tell you because, no matter how hard I tried, I couldn't stop my hands from exploring every contour of Hunt's back.

Hunt finally broke off the kiss. Still entwined, we inched a little closer to the bed. "Give yourself to me, Duncan," he whispered. "You know you want to."

And, God help me, I did.

The back of my thighs hit the foot of the bed, and we stopped and once again kissed. As his lips touched mine, I felt a sudden chill go through me, making me shiver so much that he pulled his face back, puzzled.

"What is it?"

I shook my head. "I don't know. Breeze, maybe."

The incident forgotten, Hunt smiled seductively, and reached down and shoved his briefs down. He kicked his way out of them and stood, waiting for me to do the same.

Don't look down, I told myself. *Don't look at his dick. That way lies danger.*

Dammit, my eyes didn't obey. "Whoa," I muttered. It was impressive, although I had to wonder if it was "dream sized" or actually representative of the item in question.

Again, Hunt was in my head. His eyes twinkled. "Is this a dream, though? Who's to say that it isn't any more real than what goes on when we're awake?"

I wanted to comment on that, but Hunt moved suddenly, grasping hold of me and kissing me hard. We fell back onto the bed, writhing and moaning. His hands were all over me until finally one of them found itself at my underwear, and slipped under the waistband until he got a handful of what was down there. The moans increased as my hands buried themselves in his long hair.

And then the dream exploded.

WAKING up suddenly was always a shock to the system. Waking up and finding yourself on all fours on the living room rug and feeling like a Toyota Celica not only ran over you, but somehow managed to go *through* you, was an even worse shock to the system. My brain and heart were both racing, and it took me a few moments to get my bearings.

Okay, I was alive, awake, and panting a little. Check. I was wearing the same underwear I'd gone to bed in. Check. I'd been dreaming about Dominic Hunt. Check. Oh yeah, and I still had a raging hard-on. Check. Other than that, I was flummoxed.

"You okay?"

Robbie's voice sounded close. I slowly looked up to see him standing over me, worry etched on his face.

I took a few deep breaths and tried to stand. My legs told me that wasn't such a great idea, so I sat back down on the floor and put a hand to my head to keep it from falling off. "I think so. Did someone drop a piano on me?"

"You said to stop you. I stopped you."

I groaned. My bones groaned as well. "You did at that. What happened?"

"You got up and started heading for the front door, looking like a George Romero zombie. You were even drooling. I yelled at you, but you ignored me, so I tried to tackle you. The first time I went right through you, and it barely made you pause. So I sucked up as much energy as I could and then tried again. Second time, I hit you good. I felt us collide. But then the ghost juice just sort of gave out and I fell right through you. We both ended up on the floor."

He *was* looking pretty transparent. "Thank you," I muttered.

Robbie crouched down, putting his face near mine. "Was the vampire calling you?"

"Must have been. I know I'd been dreaming about him." Not wanting Robbie to see that my shorts were tenting, I adjusted my legs so it wasn't so obvious.

Robbie reached out to stroke my hair, but stopped when he saw how vaporous he was. Neither of us would have felt a thing, other than me getting a chilled head. As it was, my body was still warming up from him battering through me. "You can't keep this up. Maybe you should take that potion Gina made for you."

I shook my head. "I got this."

"Yeah." He didn't sound convinced. "But still, why take the chance? You'll still get him. It'll just take a little longer."

I rolled my shoulders, getting the kinks out. Daisy, who had padded out of the bedroom to see what all the commotion was about, came over and licked my knee. I gave her a good petting. "It ends tonight."

Robbie frowned. "It'll be daylight in about an hour."

"I don't mean now. I mean tonight. Either he dies, or I do."

On reflection, I should have said something more confident. The worry in Robbie's eyes notched up several more levels, and I saw something in his face I don't think I've ever seen before.

He was not only worried, he was frightened.

CHAPTER 13

THE day was a windy one. The weather gurus on TV bore their serious faces and warned of possible severe thunderstorms as the day progressed. "You might want to keep the kiddies inside tonight for Halloween," the forecaster on Channel 13 had said. "Find a nice party for them to go to or something. Otherwise they might just blow away!"

For once, the weather guys hadn't been exaggerating. When I'd gone outside, I was glad I'd opted for a leather coat with a heavy lining. The trench coat, although cool, and despite what some might think, not at all Bogart-like, wouldn't have cut it.

I still wasn't feeling my best. Whether it was from being semidrained by a long-haired, fanged bastard, or because my boyfriend had rammed not only into me, but through me, I wasn't sure. I stopped at a convenience store, and for the first time in my life, bought one of those energy drinks. It tasted like shit, so it must have had some good ingredients. Ever since childhood, where my grandmother had administered cod liver oil for every ailment under the sun, I'd always had the belief that if it tastes horrible, it must be good for you. I chugged the drink, thinking, as it went down the pipes, that it must *really* have magical properties. I tossed the can into the receptacle by the exit and went back to my car, feeling much the same as I had before I'd made the stop, only $1.75 poorer.

It occurred to me that I could hit up Gina for more potions that would make me feel like ripping off my shirt à la Hulk Hogan, but I knew she'd guilt me into taking the stuff that would sever the link between me and Dominic Hunt, and I wasn't ready to give up just yet. I got back into the car and told myself I felt better, hoping mind over matter wasn't just a bunch of hooey. It seemed to work. I gunned the engine and sped out of the lot, leaving behind some tire marks on the tarmac. Nothing made you feel more bucked than driving like an asshole.

Attending the funeral of someone you'd killed was an odd experience, and I didn't recommend it. Still, when I saw the body of Matt Hamilton was being interred at Crown Hill Cemetery that afternoon, I knew I had to go. I felt I owed it to Colton Yates, and to some extent, to Matt Hamilton himself. Maybe he hadn't asked to become a vampire. Maybe he'd just been another victim. I put my guilt aside and told myself I'd saved his soul by piercing his heart with a stake. I truly believed I'd done the best thing for the young man, but that didn't mean I didn't feel like a louse for having done him in.

I arrived at the graveyard on time, but Crown Hill being a large, rambling place, it took me a few minutes to locate the area where Matt was being laid to rest. Despite the inclement weather, a large crowd had gathered to pay their last respects to the young man. I parked the car and ambled to the gravesite, not wanting to stand too close so that I felt like I was intruding, but also not wanting to be too far away and look like I was some lost soul wandering around a cemetery.

Most of the crowd huddled around the grave seemed to be younger people, probably friends who knew Hamilton from high school or because of his band. The few adults in attendance stood in a group close to the minister. A few of the women were sobbing into handkerchiefs. Standing on his own, not really with the adults and not with the younger set either, was Colton Yates. He looked pale but healthy. His eyes were dry but puffy. The poor guy looked like he was all cried out. He didn't see me as I approached the edge of the onlookers, and I didn't try to get his attention.

The minister was saying kind words about Hamilton, but he was obviously having a difficult time competing with the gusts of wind that made his speech hard to hear. He seemed to realize he was fighting a losing battle, and rushed the final few sentences out before ending with a recitation of the Lord's Prayer.

The ceremony over, the crowd began to file away. Colton, though, stayed where he was, as if unable to take his eyes from the grave. When nearly everyone else had moved away, I walked over and stood next to him.

He didn't look up, but he knew I was there. "Thank you for coming," he said quietly.

"Nearly didn't make it," I said in that reverential tone you use at funerals. "First I was over at the west end of the cemetery, where the Petersons are burying their grandmother. I gave them our condolences."

Colton cracked a slight smile. "Do you have a joke for every occasion?"

"Life's crappy. I think one needs to find as much humor as one can, whatever the situation."

"And by 'one,' you mean you."

"Well, I'm the one I know best."

The smile broadened, and now there was even a little twinkle in his eye, although the sadness was still the major tenant. "Walk me to my car?" he asked.

We slowly walked between the stones. People were still getting into their vehicles and there were lots of slamming doors, as no one wanted to linger and possibly get drenched by the downpour the sky was promising. Colton walked steadily, but his shoulders were slumped. We strode in silence for about a minute. I was trying to find appropriate words to say. On his part, he seemed to be enjoying the quiet. Well, lack of conversation. It was hardly quiet with the wind howling about our ears.

I rehearsed several speeches in my head and discarded all of them. Finally, I just said, "I owe you an apology."

"What for?"

"That night at your apartment, I wasn't very sympathetic. I know that it isn't easy to shut out a vampire's will once you've been his victim."

He looked up at my face. If he saw any confessions there, he didn't react to them. "You were trying to help me. I nearly got us both killed."

"Not your fault."

He slowed down as we approached a white Mazda that had seen better days, which I took to be his car. Colton released my elbow. "So it's over, right? Matt won't be coming back."

"No, he's at rest now."

He nodded. For a moment his face twisted, and I thought tears were about to fall, but he recovered himself. I felt like a good cry myself, but if Colton could hold his in, I could as well. "I don't know," he said, "how I can go on now with my day-to-day life, knowing that vampires and all those things that people say don't exist are really real. I'm not sure I'll ever be able to sleep easy again."

"My advice, for what it's worth, is to forget about it." Easier said than done, but he glanced up at me as if he appreciated the words. "Honestly, there are things that lurk sometimes in the dark corners, but they're few and far between. The chances of you ever coming across another living nightmare are slim. Very slim. And if you do, you call me. I'll come and take care of it for you."

"What about you?" he asked. "How do you deal with it? Knowing that these things are out there?"

"It's my life," I said. "It's what I do. I kill the monsters."

I hadn't meant that his boyfriend had been a monster, and regretted the phrase as soon as it left my mouth, but luckily he didn't seem to take offense. Instead, he smiled sadly at me. "You're like a modern-day St. George, aren't you? Slaying all the dragons that no one else sees."

Hey, I was coming up in the world. From Bogart to St. George within a twenty-four-hour period. Not bad.

BEFORE evening came, and while my mind was still 100 percent my own—or at least I told myself it was; I was still getting flashes of Hunt's face every now and then—I went to call on Nick at his apartment. I had sent him a text before heading out there, so when I knocked on the door, he wasn't surprised. He and the two cats met me at the door. Nick smiled as he ushered me in. The cats just looked haughty and circled my legs.

"Come on in," he told me. I could smell the remnants of the meal he'd just cooked for himself. I glanced over to his dining room table and saw he'd had spaghetti, which made me smile. If I survived the night, I vowed to myself to buy Nick a cookbook for Christmas. He saw my reaction and chuckled.

"I really can cook a few things other than spaghetti," he said. "Not many, but a few. I've cooked for you several times since we've met, if you'll recall!"

"Three times, I believe. Two of them were spaghetti."

"Well, you've got to go with what you know."

He offered me a drink, and I asked for a soda. While he went to the kitchen to get it, I shed my coat and settled onto the couch. Winter the cat jumped up and allowed me to stroke his back a few times. Getting all the attention he wanted, he then jumped up onto the back of the couch and settled down for a precarious nap.

I listened to the sound of ice cubes clinking in a glass, and the sound of fizz as Nick poured the drink. From the kitchen, he yelled, "I'm having wine. Are you sure you don't want some?"

"The soda will be fine," I replied. I already had weird things going on in my head. I didn't need alcohol to muddle things further. He returned, handing me a glass filled to the brim with cola. His other hand held a half-full wine glass.

"So," he asked, sitting down next to me, "what brings you out this way?"

Good question. I couldn't help feeling as if I was making my final rounds, saying good-bye to people before the sun set. It occurred to me, as I took a sip, that maybe that's what I was doing. After all, if the mental bond between Hunt and me was stronger than I believed it was, I was doomed. Despite the assurances I'd given Robbie that morning, there was a good chance Hunt would know what I had in mind, and if so, I would be dead meat. Dead meat that would then rise and want to drink some blood.

I said, "I wanted so see how you were doing. You know, with the whole ghost thing." I took a deep breath. "And... well, the letter."

Nick's cheeks flushed a deep crimson. "That was really dumb of me. I can't imagine what I was thinking."

"It's okay. Sometimes it's good to let the feelings out and not bottle them in."

"Still…. I don't really want to talk about it. Not right now, at least." He concentrated heavily on the wine glass in his hand as if it might decide to become a deadly snake at any moment. He couldn't look at me, so I let him off the hook.

"And the ghost seeing?"

"It's still up and down, I must admit, but I've decided to stay the way I am."

"You sure? Gina can easily undo what she did. All the ghosties will go away."

Nick took a large swallow of his wine. "I know. But I'll learn to live with it. Be the history teacher who talks to spirits. I may not be able to help all of them, but the ones I can…. Well, that will be rewarding."

There was something different in Nick's manner, a confidence I'd rarely seen, if ever. I arched an eyebrow. "What's happened?"

He chuckled. "Obvious, is it?" He scanned the room, as if sensing something. I could feel an energy there too, but it was very faint. "He came to me last night, or really early this morning. I got to tell him that I loved him, something that I never got to say when he was alive."

The hairs on the back of my neck bristled as the room chilled slightly and the energy increased. A faint form appeared in the room, standing a few feet away from us. He was little more than a wisp, more not there than there, but I could see it was an older man, maybe in his late fifties. I could see the smile on his face as he beamed down at Nick. The face was vaguely familiar, although I was sure I'd never seen the guy before.

"Duncan," Nick said, "I'd like to introduce you to my father. Dad, this is my friend, Duncan Andrews."

"Pleased to meet you." The words were barely a whisper in the air. Not every spirit knew the tricks Robbie knew. I nodded in greeting.

"He's going to be moving on tonight," Nick said. His eyes glistened with tears and his voice shook a little, but he continued. "We wanted to have one last conversation, though, before he left. I'm glad you're here, Duncan, so that you could meet him."

"I'm glad too." I could feel the love radiating from the spirit, even if his form was insubstantial.

"Tell your mother I love her," the spirit said. The words were getting even harder to hear.

"I will," Nick promised.

"And know," the ghost said, as he started to vanish from sight, "that I'll always love you."

And he was gone. I saw Nick's lip tremble and a single tear fall down his cheek. I put my arm around him, not knowing what else to do.

We sat like that for quite a while, neither of us speaking. It was one of those situations where words weren't needed, in any case.

CHAPTER 14

DUNCAN!

The voice was pounding in my head.

Come to meeeee!

I tried shutting out the words any way I could. I pinched the bridge of my nose. I rubbed my temples until it felt like I was pulling every hair that grew there out by the root. I bit my lip. Nothing worked.

You must come to me, Duncan!

I was sitting on my couch, but I could have been in the waiting room at Mark the Dentist's office or out in the Australian Outback, for all my surroundings mattered. I could barely see. I felt feverish. The only thing that mattered was Dominic Hunt and going to see him.

"How bad is it?"

I knew the question had been asked by Gina and that she was standing very close to me, but she sounded far off and fuzzy, as if I was hearing her over a bad telephone connection. "Wonderful," I said, hoping the sarcasm was evident. "If someone were to shoot me now, I honestly wouldn't complain."

Come to me!

I felt a cold touch on my hand. Robbie. Oh yeah, he was there too. I tried to open my eyes to see his face, but I knew I couldn't. I appreciated his touch, though. "Hang in there, Dunc," he said.

"Trying," I muttered. "It's like having a bad song stuck in your head, and that's all you can think about. Although I'd take Justin Bieber squeaking about his baby, baby, baby over this any day."

"Oh my God." I couldn't see Robbie, but I sensed him shifting his glance to Gina. "He *is* in a bad way."

That got a weak smile out of me. Was I sweating? I felt like I was sweating buckets. And I felt a nearly uncontrollable desire to get up and walk out of the apartment. Just let the voice lead me to Hunt. But I couldn't. Not yet.

"Need some mental juice here," I said. Even my own voice sounded odd, like I was under water.

Gina leaned in and placed a hand on my forehead. "Try to relax," she said.

"Easy for you to say. You don't have a foghorn going off in your brain."

"Let your mind go," she said gently. "Feel that link between you and Hunt. Let your mind travel down that link."

We were banking on the theory that, with Gina's help, the psychic link could work both ways and, if I could use my senses right, we might learn where Hunt was before I went to him. "I'm just getting darkness."

"Give it time. Let your inner eye adjust. You'll be able to see something soon."

I could see Hunt, standing at a window. The panes of the window were dirty, caked with grime, and the curtains hanging to the sides had possibly once been white, but were now gray and ripped in places. Hunt had a concerned look on his handsome face, possibly because he sensed I wasn't immediately reacting to his summons.

"I see him," I said.

Gina leaned closer, gripping my knee in excitement. "Good. Where is he?"

"A house. Someplace old, abandoned."

"Where is the house?"

"I can't tell. It's like I'm just looking in on him through a window. Like I'm standing just a few feet away."

"Move back. Think of it as astral projection, like your spiritual body can fly wherever it wants. Move away from the house."

"That would be helpful if I'd ever done astral projection before."

Gina rolled her eyes. "You really need to spend more time outside of your body."

I tried to mentally force the image I was getting in my head to move back, as if it was a camera filming some movie scene. That didn't seem to work.

Duncan, you must come to me.

And dammit, I wanted to. I wanted to feel his embrace. I wanted to feel his lips on mine. I wanted to kiss him, feel our tongues intertwine. I wanted to feel his teeth sinking into my throat. I wanted—

"You can do it, Dunc," Robbie said encouragingly.

I gritted my teeth and concentrated on the image in my head. Robbie, Gina, and the living room I was physically in seemed to melt away until all I could see was Dominic Hunt standing in some house, awaiting my arrival.

I breathed in and told myself to move back, to see more of the house. A house number. A street. Anything.

And the image of Hunt moved further away. I could now see a decrepit old house, Victorian in style and once grand, now a dingy gray derelict. Several shutters around the windows were missing, and others were askew. The porch had one pillar that had broken long ago, the middle section entirely gone. A porch swing lay lopsided, now held up on only one end by a rusted chain. A nearby window—not the one Hunt was standing at—had a busted-out pane. Several wooden steps led up to the porch. One of them was broken, leaving a jagged hole. The pillar nearest the front door had once born the house number, but all that was left was a 7, hanging nearly upside down.

"Where are you, Duncan?" Gina's voice sounded *really* far off.

You cannot resist me, Duncan. You must come to me.

I didn't know if the psychic link worked like a walkie-talkie or not, but I tried to send a message of my own into Hunt's head. *I'm coming.*

I think he got it, because the figure in the window smiled.

I closed my eyes as hard as I could and shook my head, doing my best to get his image out of my mind. I opened my eyes slowly. The link was, at least temporarily, broken. I could see Gina and Robbie standing over me.

"It's that old house in the Lockerbie area." I nodded at Robbie. "You know the one. Near the James Whitcomb Riley Museum. The local neighborhood association has been petitioning for years to get the place demolished because they think it's an eyesore, which I suppose it is, but you and I always said that when we won the lottery, we'd buy it and fix it up."

Robbie grinned slyly. "I remember the place well."

"Okay, then. I guess I'm off." I started to rise, doing so slowly to give Gina a chance to move back, as she was still nearly in my face with her hand on my knee. She didn't look happy.

"You're going unarmed? That's suicide, Duncan."

"I have to," I said. "Inside this apartment, you've got so many protection spells and hexes that he shouldn't know what we're plotting right now, but once I go out the door, that may change. Hunt may know if I'm toting a crossbow or have a handy stake in my back pocket. I can't take the chance. I'll go as I am. Besides, there's an arsenal in the car."

"But you're going to walk in empty-handed," she said, the "you're too stupid to live" part going unsaid.

"I can always nip out and grab something. Tell him I'm stepping out for a smoke." Har-har. You're a funny one, Andrews. Trying to keep the smile on my face was causing my headache to go into red-alert status.

"Let me go with you."

"Yeah, like he's not going to sense a witch in his vicinity." Vamps drew a mental blank where ghosts were concerned, but they were attuned to any other preternatural creatures.

Gina folded her arms across her chest. "I don't like this."

"Neither do I, but what the hell. Sometimes you've got to take a risk."

"That's bullshit. You're just being stubborn."

I couldn't argue with that, so I kept my clam shut. Robbie didn't look thrilled either, but he knew when I was too hopeless to argue with, so he just came close and brushed his cold lips against mine. "You take care."

"I will."

And, hopefully, I would.

I BARELY remembered the drive to the old house in Lockerbie Square. You know how sometimes you get to a destination and you have very little recollection as to how in the hell you got there? This was worse. Hunt's words and face seemed to burn in my brain. *Duncan, come to me.* Instead of seeing streetlights and other traffic, it seemed as if I had his face in front of me most of the time. Not the safest way to drive. I was an automaton, a zombie, a somnambulist. I had a brief moment of clarity when I pulled up to a red light on Tenth Street, near the Indianapolis Public Library. I realized, with some surprise, that I was managing to obey at least some of the rules of travel and wasn't just barreling through traffic signals. As I waited for the light to change, I got another vamp mental text in my head.

Duncan, you cannot resist. You must come to me.

If he could read my thoughts, and I really hoped he couldn't unless I wanted him to, he would have received a message from me. *Dude, give it a rest! I'm on my way, if I don't kill myself driving to you, because you keep popping up and filling my brain with summonses!* Vampires have no sense of self-control. With them it's all ME, ME, ME. Never a thought for the safety of their poor victim.

The thunderstorm had arrived and with it a lot of wind, making the driving even worse. Not that I was conscious of most of it. I was just assuming. Luckily, it was late, and most everybody decided they didn't want to be out driving in a deluge, so I mainly had to concentrate on staying on the road and not plowing into parked cars.

Before I knew it, I was parking my car in front of the old house in Lockerbie Square. Looking at it lit up by periodic lightning, with rain pelting against the gray structure, it looked more like something you'd see the Addams family living in, rather than a house in a fashionable district of Indianapolis. It was just as I'd seen in my vision, old and decrepit. There was even a pane knocked out of the window on the porch.

I slowly got out of the car. I'd parked with the driver's side against the curb, but I didn't think any cops coming by would want to bother to get out and get wet to cite me for improperly parking a vehicle. I also left my door open as I staggered up to the gate. The rain would soak my seat, but I could live with that as long as I lived through the next half hour. The property was surrounded by a steel fence, the only thing in good repair. The gate, thankfully, was unlocked. The squeak the hinges gave as I entered could be heard over the sound of the rain and thunder, adding to the horror-movie soundtrack already present. The rain pelted my face as I looked up to check the windows. As far as I could tell, I wasn't being watched. The inner monologue from Hunt seemed to have stopped as well. Apparently, he knew I was close.

I could, however, still feel the pull. Every fiber of my being seemed to want to get into the house as quickly as possible so I could be with Hunt. Well, nearly every fiber. Being a stubborn cuss, I ambled up the walk to the porch. Once up the steps, carefully avoiding the hole in the second one, I was partially protected by the overhang from the rain, although the wind managed to throw some my way.

Get it over with, I told myself. At least it ends now, one way or the other.

I checked the doorknob. It wasn't locked. I pushed the door open. Like the gate, it groaned eerily as it swung on its hinges.

"How cliché," I said aloud.

CHAPTER 15

I HALF expected the interior to be a scene out of a *Scooby-Doo* cartoon, with cobwebs hanging from chandeliers that might fall at any moment, and dusty portraits on the walls of previous owners, the eyes of which followed you as you moved. Instead, it was just a bare house, with not even a shred of carpet on the floors. Bare walls, bare floor, and nary a cobweb in sight. Even the spiders had vacated the place, or had retired to the basement or attic. There were plenty of mouse droppings to be seen, but no rodents came out to greet me.

I had some knowledge of the layout, as Robbie and I had been there years before, when he was still alive and kicking, with a realtor. We had really just wanted to get a peek inside the place, but we didn't let on to the stern-faced woman from Century 21 that we couldn't in our wildest dreams afford to buy the place. When we showed up and were obviously unlikely candidates, mainly because I was barely twenty at the time and Robbie even younger, I thought she would forgo showing the house to us. "I've got other properties that are probably more within your means," she had said, clearly thinking we were wasting her time. Which, in fact, we were.

In the years since, the house hadn't aged well. Perhaps the neighbors were right, and the place should just be razed to the ground to make room for some lovely overpriced condos.

A musty scent assailed my nostrils, coupled with something rancid. I'd smelled dead bodies before, and I knew there was one close by. In front of me was a staircase. With no lights on, it looked like the steps simply led to blackness. Off to my left was an archway to the living room, and as I walked further into the house, I could tell that was the source of the stench. Sure enough, as I came up to the arch, I saw the body of a young man sprawled out on the floor, his head up against the bare fireplace. Dried blood, which looked black in the meager light afforded to me, coated his neck. He didn't look like he was older than sixteen.

"He was homeless," a voice said from behind me. "Now he has a home."

I turned to see Dominic Hunt, dressed in black jeans and a dark-gray sweater, coming down the staircase. There was so little light that he appeared to glide down without the use of feet. Only the sound of the old boards of the staircase creaking under his weight belied this image. He came to the last step and stopped, putting his arms out as an indication that he wanted me to come to him.

I hesitated, glancing back at the murdered boy. "Looks like his next home should be six feet under. How long has he been here?"

If Hunt was angry that I didn't immediately fall into his embrace and bare my neck to him, he didn't show it. He smirked, pretending to ponder the boy's death. "Let's see. When did I come across our friend here? The day before yesterday? I believe so. And you of all people know that burying him would be fruitless. He should be rising soon. Tonight, I expect. And he'll be very, very thirsty. I wouldn't be standing so close to him, if I were you."

"And you just left him there?"

A slight frown crossed Hunt's brow. "Seemed a shame to go to the bother of digging a grave for him when it would only be occupied for a day or so. And he looks so comfortable there. But forget the boy."

I turned away from the youngster, my face blank. I put my arms up, as Hunt had done only moments before, beckoning him to me. "I've been looking forward to seeing you."

The frown vanished, but Hunt still looked wary. "Really? It seems to me you've been trying to fight me. You didn't come when I called you."

"I'm here now."

He still didn't come closer, hovering near the archway. "You know you can't fight me. Your blood is part of me now. We are bound together."

My lip quivered. "I admit that I tried to stay away from you. I tried to ignore you, but I couldn't. I had to come. I had to be with you. I even lied to my friends. They believe I'm here to try to destroy you."

The smirk returned. "As if you could."

"Exactly. You know I'm bound to you. You called to me, and I came." I took the few steps between us in a rush, throwing my arms around him. Our lips met, and we kissed fiercely. My tongue was in his mouth, flicking over his teeth. The fangs were present, sharp and ready. At first the passion was all on my side, but after a brief hesitation, he clasped me closer to him, holding me tight against his chest. My hands roamed along the muscles of his back and through his long hair.

He moaned, or maybe it was me.

His lips moved away from mine. He kissed my cheek, then my chin, before moving to my neck. He gently scraped his sharp teeth against the tender skin. "Are you ready? Ready to be mine for eternity?"

"The question is," I asked, "are you ready?"

Something in my tone bothered him, and he drew back, anger in his eyes. "Don't fuck with me, Duncan. I'm offering you eternal life!"

Robbie had appeared in the archway behind him, wooden stake in hand. I reached out my hand, and Robbie tossed the weapon to me.

"Trouble is," I said, "eternal life without Robbie doesn't really have that much of an appeal to me."

And, using both hands and all the strength I could muster, I shoved the stake into Hunt's chest.

Hunt gasped, staring at me uncomprehending. He hadn't sensed Robbie behind him, so to him it seemed as if I pulled the stake out of thin air. Blood began to gush out of the wound, soaking the front of his sweater. He clutched at the protruding end of the stake in a feeble attempt to pull it free. I wasn't having any of that. I shoved forward, sending both of us back into the hallway. Hunt screamed as we hit the wall. I used our momentum to drive the stake further into him. A gurgling sound erupted from his throat and blood spilled from his mouth, coating his chin and neck.

I moved away from him, and he slumped to the floor. With a dying gasp, he glanced up to see Robbie moving to my side. We put our arms around each other and watched as Hunt's skin began to blacken and peel away. His hands became gnarled claws, and then, within seconds, mere ash and bone. Hunt's jaw fell open, and his once-handsome face withered and the skin began to fall away, revealing the skull beneath.

In under a minute, we were standing over a skeleton wearing jeans and a dark, stained sweater. Then even the bones began to crack and crumble until there was just a pile of dust and clothing.

"He must have been pretty old," Robbie said quietly.

I nodded and pulled Robbie closer to me. The energy he had summoned to carry the stake from my car into the house, though, was waning, and my hand went right through him. I'd tried to make it as easy as I could for him by leaving the car door open, but his ghost batteries were still low, so to speak. "Time for him to rest," I said.

Robbie arched an eyebrow. "That was some kiss you gave him."

"Acting, dear boy. It was all acting."

Was there some jealousy in his voice? It was hard to see his face, both because of the meager light and because he was barely visible. A flash of lightning lit up the hall a little, but didn't help me decide if he was really upset. "It didn't look like acting."

"I assure you, it was. I wanted nothing more than to give you time to get in here with that stake." It had also occurred to me that, if Robbie felt some anger at seeing me smacking lips with Hunt, that would give him the extra impetus to get the stake to me ASAP. I knew it often was difficult for him to carry objects, and strong emotions gave him more psychic energy.

At least, that's what I hoped had been going through my head. I was free from Hunt's influence, but did a little bit of longing linger? Or was there some real attraction to the man?

Robbie kicked at Hunt's clothes near our feet. His sneaker just went through the pile, not even causing a flutter. "Let's get out of here."

I nodded and then looked around at the bare, grimy walls as another bolt of lightning afforded us some extra illumination. "Still want to win the lottery and buy this place?"

With a sour face, Robbie replied, "Naw. They've really let the place go to hell." He indicated the young man's body in the living room. "What about him? Should we wait to see if he vamps out, or…." He let the sentence die.

"I think we ought to satisfy the neighbors and torch the place."

I had a gas can in the trunk of the car, although it wouldn't take much for the dried-out wood to erupt into an inferno. Robbie and I walked out. I paused just outside the door and picked up the little bottle that had contained Gina's magic potion. I'd swallowed the contents before entering to ensure I wouldn't falter and fail to jab Hunt with the stake when the time came. With Hunt right there, I hadn't known if I could overcome his will unless the link was totally broken.

Minutes later, I started the car, and we drove away. I could already see the flames in the windows when we turned the corner.

CHAPTER 16

"SO YOUR obsession with Hunt," Nick said, dipping a breadstick in some marinara sauce, "was entirely due to being bitten by him." It was almost a question, and I think Nick started it off with that intent, but by the time he finished the sentence, it came out a statement.

I bought some time by fiddling my fork around in my salad. We were at the Olive Garden on Thirty-Eighth Street. The place was pretty crowded, which kept our waiter busy. That was fine with me. I hated waiters who hovered over every bite you took, filling your soda glass after you'd only taken a sip or two.

I chose my words carefully. "He was a good-looking guy, and there's something attractive, on a primal level, to vampires. There must be, or there wouldn't be hundreds of books and movies about bloodsuckers. But I think the attraction was due to the psychic link, and nothing more than that."

And that was the truth. Mostly.

Nick munched on his breadstick and thought a moment. "Why did you wait until you got to the house to drink Gina's potion? Wouldn't it have been easier to take it once you knew where he was?"

I shook my head. "I couldn't take the chance that he'd know the psychic link was broken, and then he'd be on his guard. Mind you, it would have made the drive across town easier. That was one bitch of a drive!"

"Didn't Lieutenant Carson frown over you burning the house to the ground?"

Snorting, I replied, "I didn't add that detail when I called to tell him his city was now relatively vampire free. Carson tolerates me, but I don't think he wants to know tidbits of info like that. Gives him extra paperwork and headaches." I tried some of my food. It was good, but I really wasn't hungry. "And you? How are you doing?"

Nick smiled weakly. "Still seeing the ghosts. Still dealing with them."

"And do you still feel they are better off after they've moved on?"

"I know you want me to say that I don't, but I can't say that. There's just such a feeling in the air when they've moved on, like the room is filled with happiness. I just believe that it's the right thing," he said, quickly adding, "for most of them. I'm not saying…. I mean, you and Robbie are different. But you must have felt that feeling when you helped one of them over to the other side."

"I never have."

He frowned. "Never? But you've seen ghosts all your life. Surely—"

"Okay, rarely. I've always figured it is none of my business."

Was that true? Or was I just making excuses? After all, if I truly believed that ghosts just needed a boost to cross over, then where did that leave me and Robbie? Maybe that was why I avoided dealing with spirits unless it was business related. I ignored them as much as possible. There was even one with us in the dining room at the Olive Garden, sitting alone at a table in the corner. He looked like he might have been a waiter years ago and just liked hanging out in his former workplace. I knew by his furtive glances that Nick had seen him as well, and wondered if my friend would go over after our meal was concluded and convince the guy it was okay if he said good-bye to this world.

Nick looked uncomfortable, and I wasn't feeling exactly at ease myself. Still, I went on. "Robbie's been talking about moving on."

"He's done that before."

"This time he really seems to mean it. He's thinking about leaving on New Year's Eve."

"Why then?"

I chuckled with no mirth. "I don't know. Out with the old and in with the new?"

It was the wrong thing to say. If the atmosphere at the table had been discomforting before, it was now thick and weighty. Nick's cheeks flushed slightly, and he chose to hide his embarrassment by wiping his mouth with his napkin. Carefully. I hadn't meant out with Robbie and in with Nick. Or had I? I really needed to marshal my thoughts before speaking.

After a long drink from his wine, Nick said, "That's several months away, though. It seems odd that he'd pick that date. I mean, if he really wanted to move on, if he thinks that's what he should do, why the delay? I think he just wants you to talk him out of it."

That thought had also come to me, although I'd dismissed it. Robbie had his own way of thinking and doing things, and choosing New Year's Eve seemed just like him. "I hope so," I said. "On the other hand, he might just be giving me time to get used to the idea of him not being here."

"Can't ghosts come back once they've gone to the other side? Just for a visit, like?"

I shook my head. "No."

Nick stared at his plate. He didn't look like he was hungry any longer either. "I'm sorry. I don't know what to say."

"There's nothing to say. I just thought you should know."

We finished the rest of the meal mostly in silence. *Way to kill a conversation, Andrews*, I told myself.

GINA still wasn't ready to forgive me. "You could," she said, sounding uncannily like my stern and somewhat scary third-grade teacher, "have just taken my potion right away and tracked down Hunt like you would any other vampire."

"It would have taken longer."

"Maybe. But what you did was foolhardy. What if Robbie hadn't been able to get the stake to you in time? Going in there unarmed was... beyond stupid!"

We were enjoying a fairly warm afternoon in the park, sitting on a bench, watching some boys playing soccer. The kids were mostly in shorts, taking advantage of an unseasonably mild temperature for early November. I'd left Daisy at home, which may have been a good thing. Seeing bloody squirrel corpses might have had a detrimental effect on the soccer kids.

"I knew what I was doing."

"No," Gina insisted, "you didn't."

"No," I admitted. "I didn't."

"You were just being macho and pigheaded."

"I thought that's why you liked me."

She glared at me. "Promise me you won't be that stupid next time."

"Promise." Unless, of course, the vamp made it personal by sucking my blood. And then there were the dreams, the visions I'd had. I knew that in some way, Dominic Hunt had been responsible for them, but there had still been some truth in those visions. I *did* have conflicting feelings for Nick. I *wasn't* sure being earthbound was the best thing for Robbie. And for making me see things I didn't want to face, I had wanted to kill Hunt face to face. Not by a bolt from a crossbow, or finding him during the day while he was napping and hammering a stake into him. I wanted to see the surprise in his eyes when I killed him. And I had.

I knew I should feel bad or guilty over that, but I didn't.

I hadn't told Gina about the dreams. I would never tell anyone.

She sighed and changed the subject. "How's Nick doing?"

"Good, or so he says. I had dinner with him last night. There were some dark circles under his eyes, but otherwise he looked good."

"I can always take away his ability to see spirits."

"He says he doesn't want you to. It's his new mission in life, helping souls cross over."

"And how do you feel about that?"

One of the kids scored a goal, and there was a lot of hugging and back slapping going on. They were so happy that I found myself smiling. "I'm not sure," I said, answering Gina's question after the game had resumed. "Nick insists that he feels the ghosts are much happier on the other side, and he's probably right. But it just seems like this world would be a little less mysterious and a little more sad without some spirits around to keep us guessing." I paused. "But maybe that's just me being selfish."

"Being selfish is okay," Gina said. "Selfish has a bad rep, but if you're not selfish every now and then, other people always get their way and you never do."

I lifted my face, letting the sun's rays hit it. I liked the sun. Another reason Hunt had to die. He'd been going to take the enjoyment of the sun away from me. Without permission. Bastard. "So what's your position on ghosts remaining here or passing over?"

"Mine?" She pondered that a moment. While she thought, the other team scored a goal and they engaged in revelry. When the cheering died down, she said, "I suppose it depends on the situation."

"You're not helping me make any decisions."

She looked at me. "What makes you think it's your decision to make?"

Wow. That stung. Not knowing what to look at, I gazed at my hands. There was some grit under one of my fingernails, and I tried digging it out with another fingernail. "I was talking about me and Robbie."

"I know. That's why I said it wasn't your decision."

"It's his, I know." No go with the grit. It was too embedded. "He says he'll stay until the New Year, and then he's going to go."

Gina wrapped an arm around me. Smiling gently, she asked, "Do you know what Robbie does when you're not around him?"

"I don't know. I know he watches old movies on TV sometimes."

"He does that sometimes, but there are only so many movies he can take before he's bored." The soccer ball was kicked toward us, rolling to a stop not far from the bench. A grinning, dark-haired boy ran up to retrieve it. He nodded at us and said hello. We both returned the greeting. He smacked the ball with his foot, and the game continued. Gina returned to the subject at hand. "Mostly he doesn't do anything. He just waits for you."

"He told you this?"

"He didn't have to. He's been inside my head, remember. We shared some thoughts."

It had been awhile back. Gina had been in a self-induced coma, but we needed some information from her. Since ghosts can possess people, we figured we'd try to have Robbie get into her and see if he could communicate. It had worked, which surprised the hell out of me. Ghosts and witches didn't usually mesh well.

Gina continued. "I'm sure Robbie wouldn't like me telling you this, but I think it's something you should know. He's not thinking about leaving to hurt you. Quite the contrary. He loves you more than anything. I know that without a doubt. You're his anchor. And then there's Nick."

"What about Nick?"

"He can see spirits now. He's much more a part of our little weird group. Maybe Robbie realizes that, in some way, he's not as important as he once was."

My ears burned in anger. I just wasn't sure who the anger was aimed at, Gina, Robbie, or myself. "That would never be true."

"I know that. And Robbie does too. But I think Nick's current status makes the decision a little easier for Robbie. Not that it's easy. I don't mean that. I just know that, at times, he's a very lonely spirit."

"But he always seems so happy."

"He is. When you're around." Gina sighed. "You've been his whole world for over about fifteen years now. But maybe it's not enough. Not anymore."

"So you think I should let him go?"

Gina removed her arm from around my shoulders and stood up. Looking down at me, she said, "I think you should stop believing it's something you can control. It's his decision, not yours. You have to accept that."

Suddenly the day didn't seem all that sunny. I took a deep breath. "And here I was going to try to talk him out of it."

"I think you should enjoy the time together. Know that he loves you, and always will. But goddamn it, Duncan Andrews, you've got to move on as well." She turned and walked away. I stayed put and didn't even try to hide the tear that rolled down my right cheek. If one of the soccer kids saw it, so be it.

IT WASN'T easy to surprise a ghost with a romantic dinner. While I had a sixth sense that told me when one was ready to appear, it wasn't foolproof. If I got really distracted, I didn't always pay attention to the warning signs, and one could pop up before I knew it. So while Robbie was off in the ether, building up some energy, I worked like a madman, setting the table and cooking like a demented Julia Child. Well, I say cook. Defrosting and then transferring the food onto nice plates would be a more accurate term. In no time, I was ready. I even had a tablecloth on our scratched and marred dining room table, and a single rose in a vase as a centerpiece. The candles were lit, and I'd poured the wine. Daisy watched me from her little area in the corner where she kept her stuffed animals—all of which had been gutted so that now they were just skins—as if she thought I was insane.

Done, I surveyed my work.

My reheated meal from T.G.I. Friday's was steaming on the plate. The candles cast warming shadows onto the walls. The music on the stereo was Duke Ellington. I was ready.

"Hey, Robbie," I said into the air. "You up yet?"

He appeared in the living room, a frown on his handsome face. He was wearing a beat-up football jersey and torn jeans. As I'd disturbed him during a rest, he looked like anyone else that had been roused from a slumber, with his hair disheveled, and sleepy eyes. "Something up?" he asked. And then he saw the table. "What's this?"

"This is dinner. I made it myself. Come. Sit down."

The frown deepened and then vanished, and he laughed. "You're crazy."

"Daisy thinks so too. She's been eying me warily for the last half hour. Do you like?"

Robbie came closer, taking in the steaming food and candles. "I love. It's very romantic. But I don't eat food."

"I know. That's why your plate is empty. But it was the best I could do. After dinner I thought we could take a walk down at the canal."

He seemed like he couldn't decide whether to stare uncomprehendingly at my masterwork or laugh more, so he switched on and off. "You're crazy," he repeated. "But I love it." He kissed me on the cheek. I nearly felt it. "Be right back," he said. He vanished, only to reappear moments later, now wearing a button-down shirt and jeans that didn't have rips in the knees. He was one big grin. "Shall we?"

We sat. It did feel a little odd, having a romantic dinner where one of the participants could only watch, but I hoped in this instance it really was the thought that counted. I raised my wine glass. "To us," I said.

Robbie managed to pick up his empty glass. He tilted it my way. "To us."

I picked up my fork. "Do you mind if I dig in?"

"No, please, go ahead. I love watching you eat. It's like watching Shark Week on TV. Violent and primal, yet somehow you just can't tear your eyes away."

I ate. He sat, his eyes twinkling, with his elbows on the table and his hands holding his chin. After I'd eaten in silence for a bit, I said, "I thought maybe next week we could go out of town. You know, a little vacation. Somewhere you haven't been for a while."

"We don't have too many choices. I wasn't exactly widely traveled when I was alive."

"Still, there must be some vacation spot you liked. Maybe when you were a kid."

He thought about it. "We could go camping. It might be a little cold for you—"

"Camping it is, then."

Robbie was amused, as well as mildly suspicious. "Cabin or tent?"

"Cabin, I think. It *is* November, even if it is warmer than usual right now. But you know what they say about Indiana weather. Wait a minute and it'll change. I wouldn't want to wake up in the morning and have an inch of snow on my nose."

I could see he still thought I was agreeing to this all too easily. "You're sure?"

"Sure I'm sure. When was the last time we've taken a vacation together?"

"Um… never."

That wasn't strictly true. We'd gone to King's Island in Cincinnati when Robbie had still been alive, but I wasn't going to argue the point. "Well, then we're due."

Robbie contemplated his empty plate. "Is this about—"

I cut him off. "No, it isn't. At least, not in the way you're thinking. It's not an attempt to talk you out of going."

The doubt left his face, and Robbie grinned. "Do you even know how to build a fire?"

"Can't be difficult. You get some wood and set a match to it. Easy peasy."

He chuckled. "You're going to freeze to death."

"Then we'll both be ghosts. I'm not seeing the bad side to this."

A LITTLE later, we were walking side by side along the canal. That area had undergone a lot of "urban renewal" and was now a yuppie paradise. Condos and high-end apartments now stood where once there had been warehouses. There were other couples strolling along the canal, mostly young professionals. Every now and then we'd come along a single man or woman walking a dog, but mostly we saw couples. If any of them could see a shape walking next to me, they didn't show it. I did get a few raised eyebrows from people wondering what the guy in the trench coat was doing, ambling slowly by himself along the waterside, but I ignored them. I put my hand out and Robbie grasped it, sort of. We strolled hand in almost-there hand.

"Penny for your thoughts," he said.

Did he really want to know them? For that matter, did I really know what the hell I was thinking? I was thinking so much, and not at all. I was thinking about how I might only have Robbie for another couple months. I was thinking about how my life would be if he actually decided to go. I was thinking about how I hated change. But I was thinking how nice the night was, even if a rather cool breeze had come up and made the temperature drop several degrees. I was thinking how much I loved the man beside me, and how I always would, no matter what he decided to do. I was thinking how that guy in front of us had better clean up his dog's mess, or I was going to kick his ass. But mostly I was just enjoying walking along with Robbie, enjoying the night.

"Nothing," I said.

"Nothing? There's nothing going on in your head?"

"I was just thinking how much I love you."

He stopped moving. I turned to him. We leaned in and kissed. Screw how weird it looked to the yuppies.

"I love you too," he said. "Always believe that."

And I did.

STEPHEN OSBORNE has been an improvisational comedian, a pizza restaurant manager, and a bookseller. Other than writing, his addictions include British television shows, reading mysteries, and (a recent addition) Broadway musicals. He lives in rural Illinois with Jadzia the One-Eyed Wonder Dog.

Visit him at Facebook: http://facebook.com/stephen.osborne2 and Twitter:http://twitter.com/southbendghosts. You can contact him at leftyIN@yahoo.com

The Duncan Andrews Series
from STEPHEN OSBORNE

PALE AS A GHOST

STEPHEN OSBORNE

http://www.dreamspinnerpress.com

The Duncan Andrews Series
from STEPHEN OSBORNE

ANIMAL
INSTINCT
STEPHEN OSBORNE

http://www.dreamspinnerpress.com

Also from STEPHEN OSBORNE

Pop
Goes
the
Weasel

Stephen Osborne

http://www.dreamspinnerpress.com

Also from STEPHEN OSBORNE

http://www.dreamspinnerpress.com

Also from DREAMSPINNER PRESS

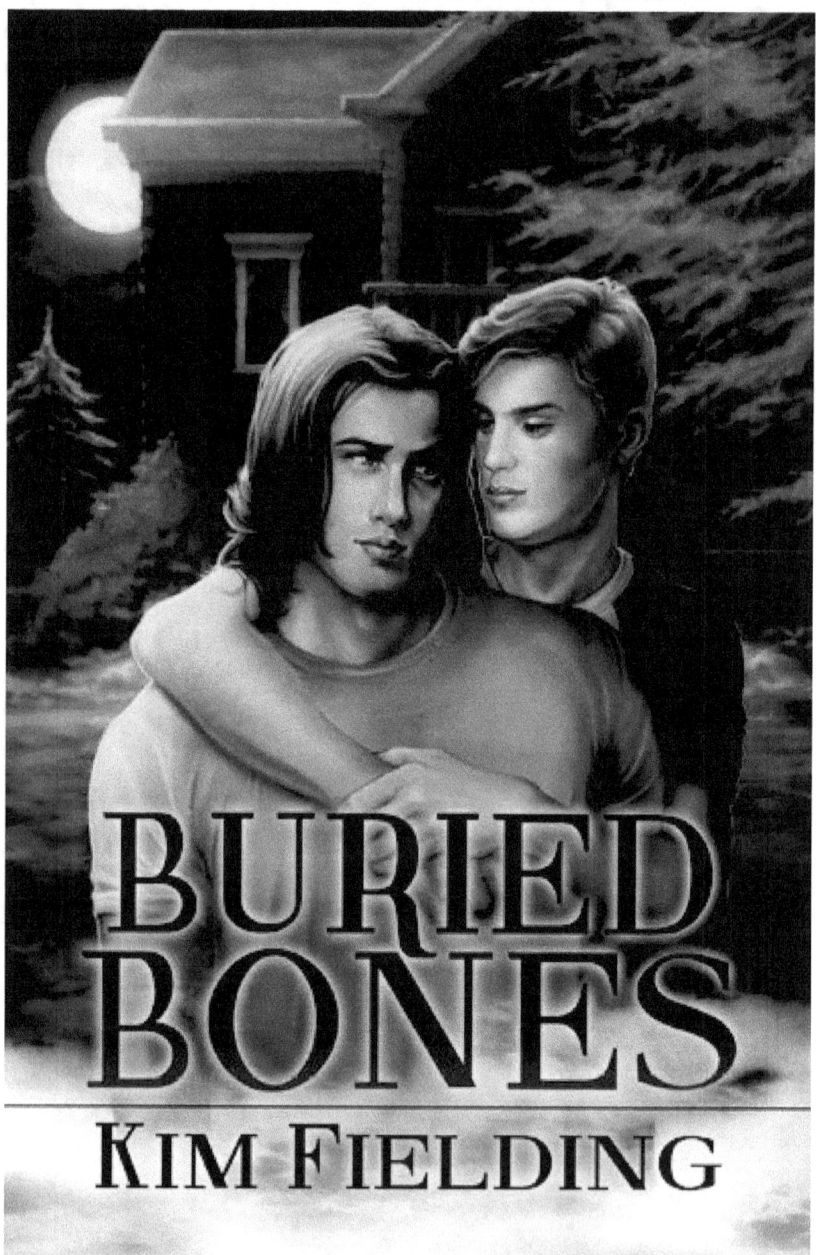

BURIED
BONES

KIM FIELDING

http://www.dreamspinnerpress.com

Also from DREAMSPINNER PRESS

http://www.dreamspinnerpress.com

Also from DREAMSPINNER PRESS

Finding a Heart of Snow

Ian Sentelik

Also from DREAMSPINNER PRESS

THE
DEMON
CATCHER

LESLEY
HASTINGS

http://www.dreamspinnerpress.com

Also from DREAMSPINNER PRESS

http://www.dreamspinnerpress.com

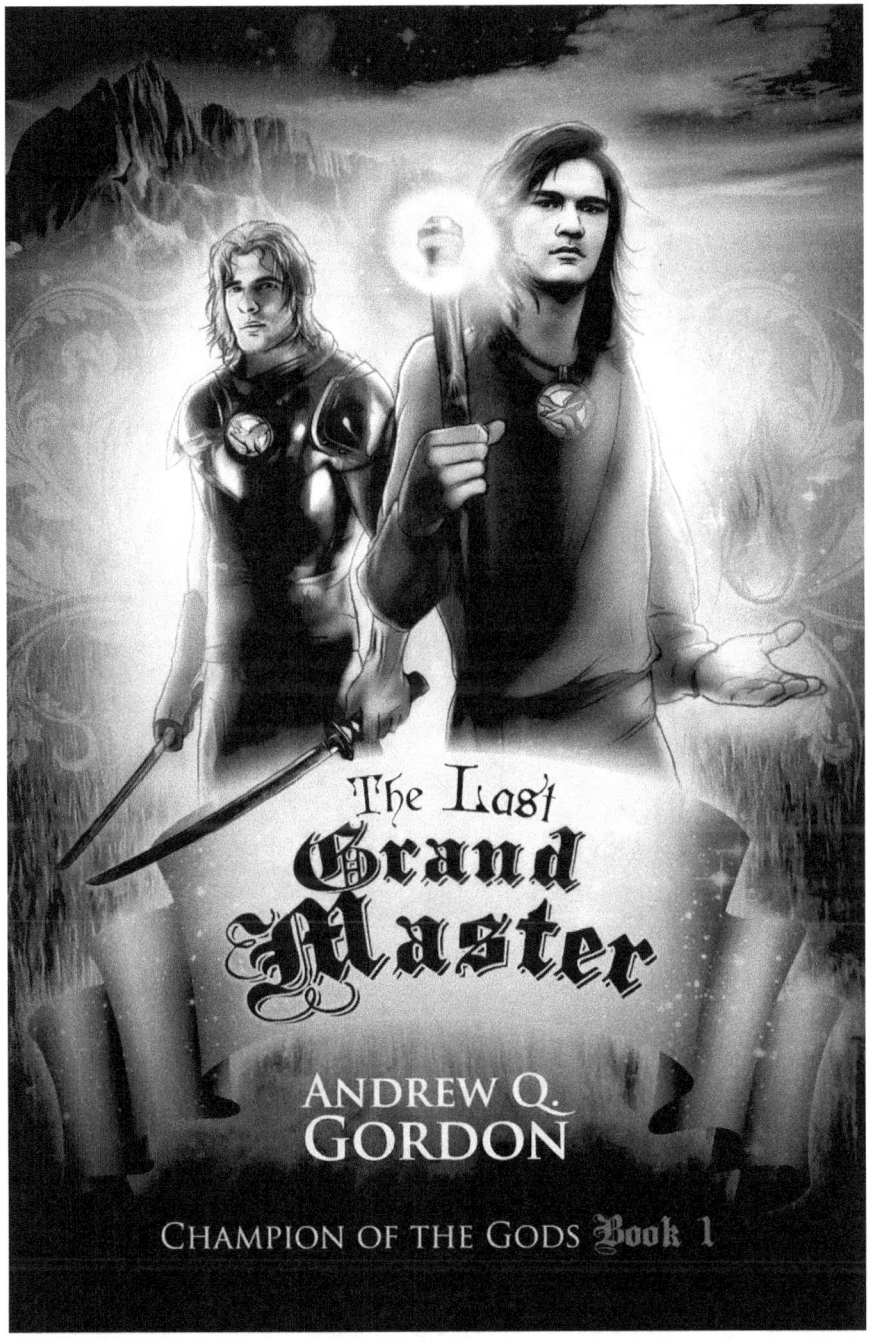

The Last
Grand
Master

ANDREW Q.
GORDON

CHAMPION OF THE GODS Book 1

www.ingramcontent.com/pod-product-compliance
Lightning Source LLC
Chambersburg PA
CBHW060103260626
47160CB00005B/1775